THE EASTER PARADE

BOOKS BY RICHARD YATES

RICHARD YATES

THE EASTER PARADE

a novel

DELTA / SEYMOUR LAWRENCE

A DELTA/SEYMOUR LAWRENCE BOOK

Published by
Dell Publishing Co., Inc.
1 Dag Hammarskjold Plaza
New York, New York 10017

Delta® TM 755118, Dell Publishing Co., Inc.

ISBN: 0-385-29283-X

Reprinted by arrangement with
Delacorte Press/Seymour Lawrence
Printed in the United States of America

First Delta printing—November 1983

To Gina Catherine

PART ONE

CHAPTER
1

Neither of the Grimes sisters would have a happy life, and looking back it always seemed that the trouble began with their parents' divorce. That happened in 1930, when Sarah was nine years old and Emily five. Their mother, who encouraged both girls to call her "Pookie," took them out of New York to a rented house in Tenafly, New Jersey, where she thought the schools would be better and where she hoped to launch a career in suburban real estate. It didn't work out—very few of her plans for independence ever did—and they left Tenafly after two years, but it was a memorable time for the girls.

"Doesn't your father ever come home?" other children would ask, and Sarah would always take the lead in explaining what a divorce was.

"Do you ever get to see him?"

"Sure we do."

"Where does he live?"

"In New York City."

"What does he do?"

"He writes headlines. He writes the headlines in the New York *Sun*." And the way she said it made clear that they ought to be impressed. Anyone could be a flashy, irresponsible reporter or a steady drudge of a rewrite man; but the man who wrote the headlines! The man who read through all the complexities of daily news to pick out salient points and who then summed everything up in a few well-chosen words, artfully composed to fit a limited space—there was a consummate journalist and a father worthy of the name.

Once, when the girls went to visit him in the city, he took them through the *Sun* plant and they saw everything.

"The first edition's ready to run," he said, "so we'll go down to the pressroom and watch that; then I'll show you around upstairs." He escorted them down an iron stairway that smelled of ink and newsprint, and out into a great underground room where the high rotary presses stood in ranks. Workmen hurried everywhere, all wearing crisp little squared-off hats made of intricately folded newspaper.

"Why do they wear those paper hats, Daddy?" Emily asked.

"Well, they'd probably tell you it's to keep the ink out of their hair, but I think they just wear 'em to look jaunty."

"What does 'jaunty' mean?"

"Oh, it means sort of like that bear of yours," he said, pointing to a garnet-studded pin in the form of a teddy bear that she'd worn on her dress that day and hoped he might notice. "That's a very jaunty bear."

They watched the curved, freshly cast metal page plates slide in on conveyor rollers to be clamped into place on the cylinders; then after a ringing of bells they watched the presses roll. The steel floor shuddered under their feet, which tickled, and the noise was so overwhelming that they couldn't talk: they could only look at each other and smile, and Emily covered her ears with her hands. White streaks of newsprint ran in every direction through the machines, and finished newspapers came riding out in neat, overlapped abundance.

"What'd you think of that?" Walter Grimes asked his daughters as they climbed the stairs. "Now we'll take a look at the city room."

It was an acre of desks, where men sat hammering type-writers. "That place up front where the desks are shoved together is the city desk," he said. "The city editor's the bald man talking on the telephone. And the man over there is even more important. He's the managing editor."

"Where's your desk, Daddy?" Sarah asked.

"Oh, I work on the copy desk. On the rim. See over there?" He pointed to a big semicircular table of yellow wood. One man sat at the hub of it and six others sat around the rim, reading or scribbling with pencils.

"Is that where you write the headlines?"

"Well, writing heads is part of it, yes. What happens is, when the reporters and rewrite men finish their stories they give them to a copy boy—that young fellow there is a copy boy—and he brings them to us. We check them over for grammar and spelling and punctuation, then we write the heads and they're ready to go. Hello, Charlie," he said to a man passing on his way to the water cooler. "Charlie, I'd like you to meet my girls. This is Sarah and this is Emily."

"Well," the man said, bending down from the waist. "What a pair of sweethearts. How do you do?"

Next he took them to the teletype room, where they could watch wire-service news coming in from all over the world, and then to the composing room where everything was set into type and fitted into page forms. "You ready for lunch?" he inquired. "Want to go to the ladies' room first?"

As they walked out across City Hall Park in the spring sunshine he held them both by the hand. They both wore light coats over their best dresses, with white socks and black patent-leather shoes, and they were nice-looking girls. Sarah was the dark one, with a look of trusting innocence that would never leave her; Emily, a head shorter, was blond and thin and very serious.

"City Hall doesn't look like much, does it?" Walter Grimes said. "But see the big building over there through the trees? The dark red one? That's the *World*—was, I should say; it folded last year. Greatest daily newspaper in America."

"Well, but the *Sun's* the best now, right?" Sarah said.

"Oh, no, honey; the *Sun* isn't really much of a paper."

"It isn't? Why?" Sarah looked worried.

"Oh, it's kind of reactionary."

"What does that mean?"

"It means very, very conservative; very Republican."

"Aren't we Republicans?"

"I guess your mother is, baby. I'm not."

"Oh."

He had two drinks before lunch, ordering ginger ale for the girls; then, when they were tucking into their chicken à la king and mashed potatoes, Emily spoke up for the first time since they'd left the office. "Daddy? If you don't like the *Sun*, why do you work there?"

His long face, which both girls considered handsome, looked tired. "Because I need a job, little rabbit," he said. "Jobs are getting hard to find. Oh, I suppose if I were very talented I might move on, but I'm just—you know—I'm only a copy-desk man."

It wasn't much to take back to Tenafly, but at least they could still say he wrote headlines.

". . . And if you think writing headlines is easy, you're wrong!" Sarah told a rude boy on the playground after school one day.

Emily, though, was a stickler for accuracy, and as soon as the boy was out of earshot she reminded her sister of the facts. "He's only a copy-desk man," she said.

Esther Grimes, or Pookie, was a small, active woman whose life seemed pledged to achieving and sustaining an elusive quality she called "flair." She pored over fashion magazines, dressed tastefully and tried many ways of fixing her hair, but her eyes remained bewildered and she never quite learned to keep her lipstick within the borders of her mouth, which gave her an air of dazed and vulnerable uncertainty. She found more flair among rich people than in the middle class, and so she aspired to the attitudes and mannerisms of wealth in raising her daughters. She always sought "nice" communities to live in, whether she could afford them or not, and she tried to be strict on matters of decorum.

"Dear, I *wish* you wouldn't do that," she said to Sarah at breakfast one morning.

"Do what?"

"Dunk your toast crusts in your milk that way."

"Oh." Sarah drew a long, soaked crust of buttered toast out of her milk glass and brought it dripping to her reaching mouth. "Why?" she asked after she'd chewed and swallowed.

"Just because. It doesn't *look* nice. Emily's four whole years younger than you, and *she* doesn't do baby things like that."

And that was another thing: she always suggested, in hundreds of ways, that Emily had more flair than Sarah.

When it became clear that she would not succeed in Tenafly real estate she began to make frequent all-day trips to other towns, or into the city, leaving the girls with other families. Sarah didn't seem to mind her absences, but Emily did: she didn't like the smells of other people's homes; she couldn't eat; she would worry all day, picturing hideous traffic accidents, and if Pookie was an hour or two late in coming to get them she would cry like a baby.

One day in the fall they went to stay with a family named Clark. They brought their paper dolls along in case they were left to themselves, which seemed likely—all three of the Clark children were boys—but Mrs. Clark had admonished her oldest son Myron to be a good host, and he took his duties seriously. He was eleven, and spent most of the day showing off for them.

"Hey, watch," he kept saying. "Watch this."

There was a horizontal steel pipe supported by steel stanchions at the far end of the Clarks' back yard, and Myron was very good at skinning-the-cat. He would run for the bar, his shirttail flapping beneath his sweater, seize it in both hands, swing his heels up under and over it and hang by the knees; then he'd reach up, turn himself inside out and drop to the ground in a puff of dust.

Later he led his brothers and the Grimes girls in a complicated game of war, after which they went indoors to examine his stamp collection, and when they came outside again there was nothing much to do.

"Hey, look," he said. "Sarah's just tall enough to go under the bar without touching it." It was true: the top of her head cleared the bar by about half an inch. "I know what let's do," Myron said. "Let's have Sarah run at the bar as fast as she can and she'll go skimming right under it, and it'll look really neat."

A distance of some thirty yards was established; the others stood on the sidelines to watch, and Sarah started to run, her long hair flying. What nobody realized was that Sarah running would be taller than Sarah standing still— Emily realized it a fraction of a second too late, when there wasn't even time to cry out. The bar caught Sarah just above the eye with a sound Emily would never forget— *ding!*—and then she was writhing and screaming in the dirt with blood all over her face.

Emily wet her pants as she raced for the house with the Clark boys. Mrs. Clark screamed a little too when she saw Sarah; then she wrapped her in a blanket—she had heard that accident victims sometimes go into shock—and drove her to the hospital, with Emily and Myron in the back seat. Sarah had stopped crying by then—she never cried much—but Emily had only begun. She cried all the way to the hospital and in the hall outside the emergency room from which Mrs. Clark emerged three times to say "No fracture" and "No concussion" and "Seven stitches."

Then they were all back at the house—"I've never seen *anyone* bear pain so well," Mrs. Clark kept saying—and Sarah was lying on the sofa in the darkened living room with most of her face swollen purple and blue, with a heavy bandage blinding one eye and a towelful of ice over the bandage. The boys were out in the yard again, but Emily wouldn't leave the living room.

"You must let your sister rest," Mrs. Clark told her. "Run along outside, now, dear."

"That's okay," Sarah said in a strange, distant voice. "She can stay."

So Emily was allowed to stay, which was probably a good thing because she would have fought and kicked if anyone had tried to remove her from where she stood on the Clarks' ugly carpet, biting her wet fist. She wasn't crying now; she was only watching her prostrate sister in the shadows and feeling wave on wave of a terrible sense of loss.

"It's okay, Emmy," Sarah said in that faraway voice. "It's okay. Don't feel bad. Pookie'll come soon."

Sarah's eye wasn't damaged—her wide, deep brown eyes remained the dominant feature in a face that would become beautiful—but for the rest of her life a fine little blue-white scar wavered down from one eyebrow into the lid, like the hesitant stroke of a pencil, and Emily could never look at it without remembering how well her sister had borne pain. It reminded her too, time and again, of her own susceptibility to panic and her unfathomable dread of being alone.

CHAPTER
2

It was Sarah who gave Emily her first information about sex. They were eating orange popsicles and fooling around a broken hammock in the yard of their house in Larchmont, New York—that was one of the other suburban towns they lived in after Tenafly—and as Emily listened her mind filled with confused and troubling images.

"And you mean they put it up *inside* you?"

"Yup. All the way. And it hurts."

"What if it doesn't fit?"

"Oh, it fits. They make it fit."

"And then what?"

"Then you have a baby. That's why you don't do it until after you're married. Except you know Elaine Simko in the eighth grade? She did it with a boy and started having a baby, and that's why she had to leave school. Nobody even knows where she is now."

"You sure? Elaine Simko?"

"Positive."

"Well, but why would she want to do a thing like that?"

"The boy seduced her."

"What does that mean?"

Sarah took a long, slow suck of her popsicle. "You're too young to understand."

"I am not. But you said it *hurts*, Sarah. If it hurts, why would she—"

"Well, it hurts, but it feels good too. You know how sometimes when you're taking a bath, or maybe you put your hand down there and kind of rub around, and it feels—"

"Oh." And Emily lowered her eyes in embarrassment. "I see."

She often said "I see" about things she didn't wholly understand—and so, for that matter, did Sarah. Neither of them understood why their mother found it necessary to change homes so often, for example—they'd be just beginning to make friends in one place when they'd move to another—but they never questioned it.

Pookie was inscrutable in many ways. "I tell my children everything," she would boast to other adults; "we don't have any secrets in this family"—and then in the next breath she would lower her voice to say something the girls weren't supposed to hear.

In keeping with the terms of the divorce agreement, Walter Grimes came out to visit the girls two or three times a year in whatever house they were renting, and sometimes he would spend the night on the living-room sofa. The year Emily was ten she lay awake for a long time on Christmas night, listening to the unaccustomed sound of her parents' voices downstairs—they were talking and talking—and because she had to know what was going on she acted like a baby: she called out for her mother.

"What is it, dear?" Pookie turned on the light and bent over her, smelling of gin.

"My stomach's upset."

"Do you want some bicarbonate?"

"No."

"What do you want, then?"

"I don't know."

"You're just being silly. Let me tuck you in, and you just think about all the nice things you got for Christmas and go to sleep. And you mustn't call me again; promise?"

"Okay."

"Because Daddy and I are having a very important talk. We're talking over a lot of things we should have discussed a long, long time ago, and we're coming to a new—a new understanding."

She gave Emily a wet kiss, turned out the light and hurried back downstairs, where the talking went on and on, and Emily lay waiting for sleep in a warm flush of happiness. Coming to a new understanding! It was like something a divorced mother in the movies might say, just before the big music comes up for the fadeout.

But the next morning unfolded like all the other last mornings of his visits: he was as quiet and polite as a stranger at breakfast, and Pookie avoided his eyes; then he called a taxi to take him to the train. At first Emily thought maybe he had only gone back to the city to get his belongings, but that hope evaporated in the days and weeks that followed. She could never find the words to ask her mother about it, and she didn't mention it to Sarah.

Both girls had what dentists call an overbite and children call buck teeth, but Sarah's condition was the worse: by the time she was fourteen she could scarcely close her lips. Walter Grimes agreed to pay for orthodontia, and this meant that Sarah rode the train into New York once a week to spend the afternoon with him, and to have her braces adjusted. Emily was jealous, both of the orthodontia and the city visits, but Pookie explained that they couldn't afford treatment for both girls at once; her turn would come later, when she was older.

In the meantime Sarah's braces were terrible: they picked up unsightly white shreds of food, and someone at school called her a walking hardware store. Who could imagine kissing a mouth like that? Who, for that matter, could bear to be close to her *body* for any length of time? Sarah washed her sweaters very carefully in an effort to keep the dyed color alive in their armpits, but it didn't work: a navy blue sweater would bleach to robin's-egg blue under the arms, and a red one to yellowish pink. Her strong sweat, no less than her braces, seemed a curse.

Another curse fell, for both girls, when Pookie announced that she'd found a wonderful house in a wonderful little town called Bradley, and that they'd be moving there in the fall. They had almost lost track of the number of times they'd moved.

"Well, it wasn't so bad, was it?" Pookie asked them after their first day of school in Bradley. "Tell me about it."

Emily had endured a day of silent hostility—one of the only two new girls in the whole sixth grade—and said she guessed it had been all right. But Sarah, a high-school freshman, was bubbling over with news of how fine it had been.

"They had a special assembly for all the new girls," she

said, "and somebody played the piano and all the old girls stood up and sang this song. Listen:

> How do you do, new girls, how do you do?
> Is there anything that we can do for you?
> We are glad that you are here
> For you always bring good cheer
> How do you do, new girls, how do you do?"

"Well!" Pookie said happily. "Wasn't that nice."

And Emily could only turn her face away in a spasm of disgust. It may have been "nice," but it was treacherous; *she* knew the treachery implicit in a song like that.

The grade school and high school were in the same big building, which meant that Emily could catch occasional glimpses of her sister, if she was lucky, during the day; it also meant they could walk home together every afternoon. The arrangement was that they would meet in Emily's classroom after school.

But one Friday during football season Emily found herself waiting and waiting in the empty classroom, with no sign of Sarah, until her stomach began to knot with anxiety. When Sarah did arrive at last she looked funny—she had a funny smile—and behind her lumbered a frowning boy.

"Emmy, this is Harold Schneider," she said.

"Hi."

"Hi." He was big and muscular and pimple-faced.

"We're going to the game over in Armonk," Sarah explained. "Just tell Pookie I'll be home for dinner, okay? You won't mind walking home by yourself, will you?"

The trouble was that Pookie had gone into New York that morning, after saying, at breakfast, "Well, I *think* I'll get home before you do, but I'd better not promise." That meant not only walking home alone but letting herself into the empty house alone to stare for hours at the naked furniture and the ticking clock, waiting. And if her mother ever did come home—"Where's Sarah?"—how could she ever tell her that Sarah had gone off with a boy named Harold to a town called Armonk? It was out of the question.

"How're you gonna get there?" she inquired.

"In Harold's car. He's seventeen."

"I don't think Pookie'd like that, Sarah. And I think you know she wouldn't like it. You better come on home with me."

Sarah turned helplessly to Harold, whose big face had twitched into a half-smile of incredulity, as if to say he'd never met such a bratty little kid in his life.

"Emmy, don't *be* this way," Sarah implored, with a quaver that proved she was losing the argument.

"Be *what* way? I'm only saying what you know."

And in the end Emily won. Harold Schneider slouched away down the hall, shaking his head (he could probably find another girl before game time), and the Grimes sisters walked home together—or rather in single file, with Emily in the lead.

"Damn you, damn you, damn you," Sarah said behind her on the sidewalk. "I could *kill* you for this—" and she took three running steps and kicked her little sister solidly on one buttock, causing Emily to fall on her hands and spill all her schoolbooks, the loose-leaf binder breaking open and scattering its pages. "—I could *kill* you for ruining everything."

It turned out, ironically, that Pookie was home when they got there. "What's the *matter*?" she asked, and when Sarah had told the whole story, crying—it was one of the very few times Emily had ever seen her cry—it became clear that all the mistakes of the afternoon had been Emily's.

"And were there a lot of people going to the game, Sarah?" Pookie inquired.

"Oh, yes. All the seniors and everybody . . ."

Pookie looked less bewildered than usual. "Well, Emily," she said sternly. "That wasn't good at all, what you did. Do you understand that? It wasn't good at all."

There were better times in Bradley. That winter Emily made a few friends with whom she fooled around after school, which tended to make her worry less about whether Pookie would be home or not; and during that same winter Harold Schneider began taking Sarah to the movies.

"Has he kissed you yet?" Emily inquired after their third or fourth date.

"None of your business."

"Come on, Sarah."

"Oh, all right. Yes. He has."

"What's it like?"

"It's about like what you'd imagine."

"Oh." And Emily wanted to say Doesn't he mind your braces? but thought better of it. Instead she said "What do you see in Harold, anyway?"

"Oh, he's—very nice," Sarah said, and went back to washing her sweater.

There was another town after Bradley, and then still another; in the last town Sarah graduated from high school with no particular plans for college, which her parents couldn't have afforded anyway. Her teeth were straight now and the braces had come off; she seemed never to sweat at all, and she had a lovely full-breasted figure that made men turn around on the street and made Emily weak with envy. Emily's own teeth were still slightly bucked and would never be corrected (her mother had forgotten her promise); she was tall and thin and small in the chest. "You have a coltish grace, dear," her mother assured her. "You'll be *very* attractive."

In 1940 they moved back to the city, and the place Pookie found for them was no ordinary apartment: it was a once-grand, shabby old "floor through" on the south side of Washington Square, with big windows facing the park. It cost more than Pookie could afford, but she scrimped on other expenses; they bought no new clothes and ate a great deal of spaghetti. The kitchen and bathroom fixtures were rusty antiques, but the ceilings were uncommonly high and visitors never failed to remark that the place had "character." It was on the ground floor, which meant that passengers on the double-decked Fifth Avenue buses could peer into it as they made their circuit of the park on the way uptown, and there seemed to be a certain amount of flair in this for Pookie.

Wendell L. Willkie was the Republican candidate for President that year, and Pookie sent the girls uptown to work as volunteers in the national headquarters of something called Associated Willkie Clubs of America. She thought it might be good for Emily, who needed something to do; more importantly, she thought it would give Sarah a chance to "meet people," by which she meant suitable young men. Sarah was nineteen, and none of the boys she'd liked so far, from Harold Schneider on, had struck her mother as suitable at all.

Sarah did meet people at the Willkie Clubs; within a few weeks she brought home a young man named Donald

Clellon. He was pale and very polite, and dressed so carefully that the first thing you noticed about him was his clothes: a pinstripe suit, a black Chesterfield with a velvet collar, and a black derby. The derby was a little odd—they hadn't been in style for years—but he wore it with such authority as to suggest that the fashion might be coming back. And he spoke in the same meticulous, almost fussy way he dressed: instead of saying "something like that" he always said "something of that nature."

"What do you see in Donald, anyway?" Emily asked.

"He's very mature and very considerate," Sarah said. "And he's very—I don't know, I just like him." She paused and lowered her eyes like a movie star in a close-up. "I think I may be in love with him."

Pookie liked him well enough too, at first—it was charming for Sarah to have such an attentive suitor—and when they solemnly asked her permission to become engaged she cried a little but raised no objection.

It was Walter Grimes, to whom the engagement was presented as an accomplished fact, who asked all the questions. Who exactly *was* this Donald Clellon? If he was twenty-seven, as he claimed, what business or profession had he been in before the Willkie campaign? If he was as well-educated as his manner implied, where had he gone to college? Where, for that matter, was he from?

"Why didn't you just ask him, Walter?"

"I didn't want to grill the kid over a lunch table, with Sarah sitting there; I thought you'd probably have the answers."

"Oh."

"You mean you've never asked him anything either?"

"Well, he's always seemed so—no; I haven't."

There followed several tense interviews, usually late at night after Pookie had waited up for them, with Emily listening just outside the living-room door.

"... Donald, there's something I've never quite understood. Where exactly are you from?"

"I've told you, Mrs. Grimes. I was born here in Garden City but my parents moved around quite a lot. I was raised chiefly in the Middle West. Various parts of the Middle West. After my father died my mother moved to Topeka, Kansas; that's where she makes her home now."

"And where did you go to college?"

"I thought I'd told you that too, when we first met. The fact is I haven't been to college; we couldn't afford it. I was fortunate enough to find work in a law firm in Topeka; then after Mr. Willkie's nomination I worked for the Willkie Club out there until I was transferred here."

"Oh. I see."

And that seemed to take care of it for one night, but there were others.

"... Donald, if you only worked in the law office for three years, and if you went there right after high school, then how can you be—"

"Oh, it wasn't right after high school, Mrs. Grimes. I held a number of other jobs first. Construction work, heavy laboring jobs, things of that nature. Anything I could get. I had my mother to support, you see."

"I see."

In the end, after Willkie had lost the election and Donald was working at some vague job with a brokerage house downtown, he contradicted himself enough times to reveal that he wasn't twenty-seven; he was twenty-one. He'd been exaggerating his age for some time because he'd always *felt* older than his contemporaries; everyone in the Willkie

Clubs had thought he was twenty-seven, and when he'd met Sarah he'd said "twenty-seven" automatically. Couldn't Mrs. Grimes understand an indiscretion like that? Couldn't Sarah understand?

"Well, but Donald," Pookie said, while Emily strained to hear every nuance of the talk, "if you haven't told the truth about that, how can we trust you about anything else?"

"How can you trust me? Well, you know I love Sarah; you know I have a good future in the brokerage business—"

"How do we know that? No, Donald, this won't do. It won't do at all . . ."

After their voices stopped, Emily risked a peek into the living room. Pookie looked righteous and Sarah looked stricken; Donald Clellon sat alone with his head in his hands. There was a little ridge around the crown of his well-combed, brilliantined hair, marking the place where his derby had been.

Sarah didn't bring him home again, but she continued to meet and go out with him several times a week. The heroines of all the movies she had ever seen made clear that she couldn't do otherwise; besides, what about all the people to whom she'd introduced him as "my fiancé"?

". . . He's a liar!" Pookie would shout. "He's a child! We don't even know *what* he is!"

"I don't *care*," Sarah would shout back. "I love Donald and I'm going to marry him!"

And there would be nothing for Pookie to do but flap her hands and cry. The quarrels usually ended with both of them collapsed in tears in different parts of the musty, elegant old apartment, while Emily listened and sucked her knuckles.

But everything changed with the coming of the new year: a family moved in upstairs that Pookie found immediately interesting. Their name was Wilson, a middle-aged couple with a grown son, and they were English war refugees. They had been through the London Blitz (Geoffrey Wilson was too reserved to talk much about it, but his wife Edna could tell dreadful stories), and they'd escaped to this country with only the clothes on their backs and whatever they could carry in their suitcases. That was all Pookie knew about them at first, but she was careful to linger around the mailboxes in the hope of striking up further conversations, and it wasn't long before she knew more.

"The Wilsons aren't really English at all," she told her daughters. "You'd never guess it from their accents, but they're Americans. He's from New York—he comes from an old New York family—and she's a Tate from Boston. They went to England many years ago for his business— he was the British representative for an American firm— and Tony was born there and went to an English public school. That's what the English call their private boarding schools, you know. I just knew he'd been to an English public school because of the delightful way he talks—he says 'I say,' and 'Oh, rot,' and things like that. Anyway, they're wonderful people. Have you talked to them yet, Sarah? Have you, Emmy? I *know* you'd both love them. They're so—I don't know, so wonderfully *English*."

Sarah listened patiently enough, but she wasn't interested. The strain of her engagement to Donald Clellon was beginning to show: she was very pale, and she'd lost weight. Through people in the Willkie campaign she had found work for a token salary in the offices of United China Relief; she was called Chairman of the Debutante

Committee, a title Pookie loved to pronounce, and her job was to supervise the rich girls who volunteered to collect nickels and dimes along Fifth Avenue to help the Chinese multitudes in their war against the Japanese. The work wasn't hard but she came home exhausted every night, sometimes too tired even to go out with Donald, and she spent much of her time in a brooding silence that neither Pookie nor Emily could penetrate.

And then it happened. Young Tony Wilson came hurrying downstairs one morning, his fine English shoes barely touching the tread of each warped step, just as Sarah walked out into the vestibule, and they almost collided.

"Excuse me," she said.

"Excuse *me*. Are you Miss Grimes?"

"Yes. And you're—"

"Tony Wilson; I live upstairs."

Their talk couldn't have lasted more than three or four minutes before he excused himself again and left the house, but it was enough to bring Sarah sleepwalking back into the apartment, allowing herself to be late for work. The debutantes and the Chinese multitudes could wait. "Oh, Emmy," she said, "have you *seen* him?"

"I've passed him in the hall occasionally."

"Well, isn't he something? Isn't he just about the most— the most beautiful person you've ever—"

Pookie came into the living room, her eyes wide and her uncertain lips glistening with breakfast bacon grease. "Who?" she said. "You mean Tony? Oh, I'm so glad; I knew you'd like him, dear."

And Sarah had to sit down in one of their moth-eaten easy chairs to catch her breath. "Oh, Pookie," she said. "He looks—he looks just like Laurence Ol*iv*ier."

That was true, though Emily hadn't thought of it before.

Tony Wilson was of medium height, broad-shouldered and well-built; his wavy brown hair was carelessly arranged across the forehead and around the ears; his mouth was full and humorous and his eyes seemed always to be laughing at some subtle private joke that he might tell you when you got to know him better. He was twenty-three years old.

A very few days later he knocked on the door to ask if he might have the pleasure of Sarah's company for dinner some evening soon, and that was the end of Donald Clellon.

Tony didn't have much money—"I'm a laborer," he said, which meant that he worked at a big naval aircraft plant on Long Island and very likely did something of Top Secret importance—but he owned a 1929 Oldsmobile convertible and drove it with flair. He would take Sarah on drives into the far reaches of Long Island or Connecticut or New Jersey, where they'd have dinner at what she always described as "wonderful" restaurants, and they'd always be back in time for a drink at a "wonderful" bar called Anatole's, which Tony had discovered on the upper East Side.

"Now, *this* fellow's a different story entirely," Walter Grimes said on the telephone. "I like him; you can't help liking him . . ."

"Our young people seem to be getting on rather well, Mrs. Grimes," Geoffrey Wilson said one afternoon, with his wife smiling beside him. "Perhaps it's time for *us* to get better acquainted."

Emily had often seen her mother flirt with men before, but never quite so openly as the way she flirted with Geoffrey Wilson. "Oh, that's *marvelous!*" she would cry at his every minor witticism, and then she'd dissolve into peals of deep-throated laughter, pressing her middle finger coquettishly against her upper lip to conceal the fact that her gums were shrinking and her teeth going bad.

And Emily thought the man *was* funny—it wasn't so much what he said, she decided, as the way he said it—but she was embarrassed by Pookie's enthusiasm. Besides, a little too much of Geoffrey Wilson's humor depended on his strange delivery, in which the heavy English accent seemed compounded by a speech impediment: he talked as though he held a billiard ball in his mouth. His wife Edna was pleasant and plump and drank a good deal of sherry.

Emily was always included in her mother's afternoons and evenings with the Wilsons—she would sit quietly and nibble salted crackers through their talk and laughter—but she would much rather have been out with Sarah and Tony, riding in that splendid old car with her hair blowing attractively in the wind, strolling with them along some deserted beach and then coming back to Manhattan at midnight and sitting in their special booth at Anatole's while the pianist played their song.

"Do you and Tony have a song?" she asked Sarah.

"A song?" Sarah was painting her fingernails, and she was in a hurry because Tony would call for her in fifteen minutes. "Well, Tony likes 'Bewitched, Bothered and Bewildered,' but I sort of like 'All the Things You Are.'"

"Oh," Emily said, and now she had music to accompany her fantasies. "Well, they're both good songs."

"And you know what we do?"

"What?"

"Well, when we're having our first drink we kind of hook our arms around each other's like this—here, I'll show you. Careful of my nails." And she slipped her wrist through the crook of Emily's elbow and brought an imaginary glass to her own lips. "Like that. Isn't that nice?"

It certainly was. Everything about Sarah's romance with Tony was almost too nice to be borne.

"Sarah?"

"Mm?"

"Would you go all the way with him if he asked you to?"

"You mean before we're married? Oh, Emily, don't be ridiculous."

So it wasn't quite as profound a romance as some she'd read about, but even so it was very, very nice. That night Emily lay steaming in her bath for a long time, and when she'd gotten out and dried herself, with the bathwater slowly draining away, she stood posing naked at the mirror. Because her breasts were so meager she concentrated on the beauty of her shoulders and her neck. She pouted and parted her lips very slightly, the way girls did in the movies when they were just about to be kissed.

"Oh, you're lovely," said a phantom young man with an English accent, just out of camera range. "I've wanted to say this for days, for weeks, and now I must: it's you I love, Emily."

"I love you too, Tony," she whispered, and her nipples began to harden and rise of their own accord. Somewhere in the background a small orchestra played "All the Things You Are."

"I want to hold you. Oh, let me hold you and I'll never let you go."

"Oh," she whispered. "Oh, Tony."

"I need you, Emily. Will you—will you go all the way with me?"

"Yes. Oh, yes, Tony, I will. I will . . ."

"Emmy?" her mother called from outside the locked

door. "You've been in that bathroom over an *hour*. What're you *doing* in there?"

At Easter time Sarah's employers lent her an expensive dress of heavy silk, said to be a model of the kind of clothes worn by aristocratic Chinese ladies before the war, and a broad-brimmed hat of closely woven straw. Her assignment was to mingle with the fashionable crowds on upper Fifth Avenue and to get her picture taken by a photographer from the public relations office.

"Oh, you look stunning, dear," Pookie said on Easter morning. "I've never seen you look so lovely."

But Sarah only frowned, which made her all the lovelier. "I don't *care* about the silly Easter parade," she said. "Tony and I were planning to drive out to Amagansett today."

"Oh, please," Pookie said. "It'll only be for an hour or two; Tony won't mind."

Then Tony came in and said "Oh, I say. Smashing." And after looking at Sarah for a long time he said "Look; I've an idea. Can you wait five minutes?"

They heard him charge upstairs, seeming to shake the old house, and when he came back he was wearing an English cutaway, complete with flowing ascot, dove-gray waistcoat and striped trousers.

"Oh, Tony," Sarah said.

"It wants a pressing," he said, turning around for their admiration and shooting his cuffs, "and one really ought to have a gray topper, but I think it'll do. Ready?"

Emily and Pookie watched from the windows as the open car rolled past on its way uptown—Tony turning briefly from the wheel to smile at them, Sarah holding her hat in place with one hand and waving with the other— and then they were gone.

The public relations photographer did his job well, and

so did the editors of the rotogravure section of *The New York Times*. The picture came out the following Sunday in a pageful of other, less striking photographs. The camera had caught Sarah and Tony smiling at each other like the very soul of romance in the April sunshine, with massed trees and a high corner of the Plaza hotel just visible behind them.

"I can get eight-by-ten glossies from the office," Sarah said.

"Oh, wonderful," Pookie said. "Get as many as you can. And let's get more newspapers, too. Emmy? Get some money out of my purse. Run down to the newsstand and get four more papers. Get six."

"I can't carry that many."

"Of course you can."

And whether she was annoyed or not as she left the house, Emily knew how important it was to have as many copies as possible. It was a picture that could be mounted and framed and treasured forever.

CHAPTER 3

They were married in the fall of 1941, in a small Episcopal church of Pookie's choosing. Emily thought the wedding was nice enough, except that the dress she had to wear as bridesmaid seemed contrived to call attention to her small breasts, and also that her mother wept throughout the ceremony. Pookie had spent a lot of money on her own dress and rich little hat, both in a new shade called Shocking Pink, and she'd spent many days regaling anyone who would listen with the same weak joke. "How would *that* look in the newspapers?" she asked time and again, pressing her middle finger to her upper lip. " 'The bride's mother wore Shocking Pink!' " She drank too much at the reception, too, and when the time came for her to dance with Geoffrey Wilson she batted her eyelids and sank as dreamily into his arms as if it were he and not his son who looked like Laurence Olivier. He was visibly embarrassed and tried to loosen his hold on her back, but she clung to him like a slug.

Walter Grimes kept mostly to himself at the party; he stood nursing his scotch, ready to smile at Sarah whenever she smiled at him.

Sarah and Tony went to Cape Cod for a week, while Emily lay worrying about them. (What if Sarah was too nervous to do it right the first time? And if it wasn't right the first time, what could you possibly talk about while you waited to try again? And if it became a matter of trying, wouldn't that spoil everything?) Then they settled into what Pookie described as a "wretched little apartment" near the Magnum Aircraft plant.

"But that's only temporary," she would tell her friends on the telephone. "In a few months they'll be moving into the Wilsons' estate. Have I told you about the Wilsons' estate?"

Geoffrey Wilson had inherited, from his father, eight acres of land in the hamlet of St. Charles, on the North Shore of Long Island. The place had a fourteen-room main house (Pookie always described it as "a wonderful old house," though she hadn't yet seen it); that was where Geoffrey and Edna would live as soon as the present tenants' lease expired next year. And there was a separate cottage on the property that would be perfect for Sarah and Tony; didn't that sound like the ideal arrangement?

Pookie talked so much about the Wilsons' estate all winter that she seemed scarcely to realize the war had started, but Emily realized almost nothing else. Tony was an American citizen, after all; he would probably be drafted and trained and sent somewhere to have his handsome head blown off.

"Tony says it's nothing to worry about," Sarah assured

her, one day when Emily and Pookie went out to visit the "wretched" apartment. "Even if he *is* drafted he's pretty sure the higher-ups at Magnum will arrange to get him assigned back to the plant as enlisted naval personnel. Because Tony doesn't just *work* at Magnum; he's practically an engineer. He had almost three years' apprenticeship with an engineering firm in England—that's the way they do it over there, you see, they have apprenticeships instead of engineering school—and the people at Magnum realize that. He's a valuable man."

He didn't look very valuable when he came home from the plant that afternoon, wearing green work clothes with an employee identification badge clipped over his heart, carrying his tin lunch box under his arm, but despite that costume he managed to radiate the old elegant vigor and charm. Maybe Sarah was right.

"I say," he said. "Won't you join us for a drink?"

He and Sarah sat close together on the sofa and carefully went through the ritual from Anatole's, entwining their arms to take the first sip.

"Do you always do that?" Emily inquired.

"Always," Sarah said.

That spring Emily was awarded a full scholarship to Barnard College.

"Wonderful!" Pookie said. "Oh, darling, I'm so proud of you. Just think: you'll be the first member of our family with a college education."

"Except for Daddy, you mean."

"Oh. Well, yes, I suppose that's right; but I meant *our* family. Anyway, it's just wonderful. Tell you what let's do. Let's call Sarah right away and tell her, and then you and I'll get all dolled up and go out and celebrate."

They did call Sarah—she said she was very pleased—
and then Emily said "I'm going to call Daddy now, okay?"

"Oh. Well, all right, certainly, if you want to."

". . . A *full* scholarship?" he said. "Wow. You must have
really impressed those people . . ."

She arranged to meet him for lunch the following day,
in one of the dark basement restaurants he liked near
City Hall. She got there first and waited near the coatroom,
and she thought he looked surprisingly old as he came
down the steps, wearing a raincoat that wasn't quite clean.

"Hello, honey," he said. "My God, you're getting tall.
We'd like a booth for two, George."

"Certainly, Mr. Grimes."

And maybe he was only a copy-desk man, but the head-
waiter knew his name. The waiter knew him too—knew
just which kind of whiskey to bring and set before him.

"That's really great about Barnard," he said. "It's the
best news I've had in I don't know how long." Then he
coughed and said "Excuse me."

The drink brightened him—his eyes shone and his mouth
tightened pleasantly—and he had a second one before the
food arrived.

"Did you go through Syracuse on a scholarship, Daddy?"
she asked, "Or did you pay your way?"

He looked puzzled. " 'Go through Syracuse?' Honey, I
didn't 'go through.' I only went to Syracuse for a year, then
I started working on the town paper up there."

"Oh."

"You mean you thought I was a college graduate?
Where'd you get that idea? Your mother?"

"I guess so, yes."

"Well, your mother has her own way of dealing with information."

He didn't eat all of his lunch, and when the coffee came he peered down at it as if it didn't appeal to him either. "I wish Sarah could have gone to college," he said. "Of course it's fine that she's happily married, and all that, but still. Education is a wonderful thing." Then the cough hit him again. He had to turn away from the table and press a handkerchief to his mouth and nose, and a small vein stood out in his temple as he coughed and coughed. When it was over, or nearly over, he reached for his water glass and took a sip. That seemed to help—he was able to take several deep breaths—but then his breath caught and he was coughing again.

"You do have a bad cold," she said when he'd recovered.

"Oh, it's only partly the cold; it's mainly the damn cigarettes. You know something? Twenty years from now cigarettes'll be against the law. People'll have to get them from bootleggers, the way we did with liquor during Prohibition. Have you thought about what you'll major in?"

"English, I think."

"Good. You'll read a lot of good books. Oh, you'll read some that aren't so good, too, but you'll learn to distinguish between them. You'll live in the world of ideas for four whole years before you have to concern yourself with anything as trivial as the demands of workaday reality—that's what's nice about college. Would you like some dessert, little rabbit?"

When she got home that day she thought of facing down her mother with the truth about Syracuse, but decided against it. There was no hope of changing Pookie.

Nor was there any hope, it seemed, of changing the way they had come to spend their evenings together since Sarah's marriage. Occasionally the Wilsons would invite them upstairs, or come down; more often the two of them sat reading magazines in the living room, while cars and Fifth Avenue buses droned past the windows. One or the other of them might make a plate of fudge, more to kill time than to satisfy any real craving, and on Sundays there were good programs on the radio, but for the most part they were as idle as if they had nothing to do but wait for the telephone to ring. And what could be less likely than that? Who would want to call up an aging divorcée with rotten teeth, or a plain, skinny girl who moped around feeling sorry for herself all the time?

One night Emily spent half an hour watching her mother turn the pages of a magazine. Pookie would slowly, absently wipe her thumb against her moist lower lip and then wipe the thumb against the lower right-hand corner of each page, for easier turning; it left the corners of all the pages wrinkled and faintly smeared with lipstick. And tonight she had eaten fudge, which meant there would be traces of fudge as well as lipstick on the pages. Emily found she couldn't watch the process without grinding her teeth. It made her scalp prickle too, and made her squirm in her chair. She got up.

"I think I'll go to a movie," she said. "There's supposed to be a fairly good one at the Eighth Street Playhouse."

"Oh. Well, all right, dear, if you want to."

She escaped to the bathroom to comb her hair, and then she was free of the house, walking out into Washington Square, taking deep breaths of the gentle air and taking a small but honest pride in the fit and hang of her almost-new yellow dress. It was just after dark and the park lamps were glowing in the trees.

"Excuse me, miss," said a tall soldier walking beside her. "Can you tell me where Nick's is? The jazz place?"

And she stopped in perplexity. "Well, I know where it is—I mean I've been there a few times—but it's sort of hard to tell you how to get there from here. I guess the best thing would be to go down Waverly to Sixth Avenue, no, Seventh Avenue, and then turn left—I mean right—and go uptown about four or five—no, wait; your quickest way would be to go down Eighth Street to Greenwich Avenue; that'll take you . . ."

And the whole time she was babbling that way, waving her hands to make inaccurate directions, he stood smiling patiently down at her. He was a homely boy with kind eyes, and he looked very trim in his bright tan summer uniform.

"Thanks," he said when she was finished. "But I got a better idea. How'd you like to take a ride on a Fifth Avenue bus?"

Climbing the steep, curved staircase of an open-topped double-decker had never before seemed the beginning of a perilous adventure, nor had it ever made her aware of the pump of her heart. When they rode past her house she shrank away from the railing and averted her face in case Pookie happened to be looking out the window.

One lucky thing was that the soldier did most of the talking. His name was either Warren Maddock or Warren Maddox—she would have to ask him to clear that up later. He was on a three-day pass from Camp Croft, South Carolina, where he had completed infantry training, and he would soon be "shipped out to a division," whatever that meant. His home was a small town in Wisconsin; he was the oldest of four brothers, and his father was in the roofing business. This was his first visit to New York.

"You lived here all your life, Emily?"

"No; I lived mostly in the suburbs."

"I see. Must be funny for a person to live here all their life, never get a chance to get out and run or anything. I mean it's a great city, don't get me wrong; I just mean I think the country's better for growing up. You in high school?"

"Not any more. I'm going to Barnard College in the fall." After a moment she added "I have a scholarship there."

"A scholarship! Hey, you must be smart. I better watch my step around a girl like you." And with that he let his hand slip from the wooden back of the seat to hold her shoulder; his big thumb began massaging the flesh near her collarbone as he talked.

"What kind of work's your dad do?"

"He's a newspaperman."

"Oh yeah? Is that the Empire State Building up ahead?"

"Yes."

"I thought so. Funny, I've seen pictures of it, but you don't really get the idea how big it is. You've got nice hair, Emily. I never have much liked curly hair on a girl; straight hair's a lot nicer . . ."

Somewhere above Forty-second Street he kissed her. It wasn't the first time she'd been kissed—not even the first time she'd been kissed on top of a Fifth Avenue bus; one of the boys in high school had been that brave—but it was the first kiss of its kind, ever.

At Fifty-ninth he mumbled "Let's take a walk," and helped her down the rumbling stairs; then they were in Central Park, and his arm was still around her. This part of the park was crawling with soldiers and girls: they sat necking on benches, and they walked in groups or in couples with their arms around each other. Some of the walking girls had let their fingers slip into their soldiers' hip pockets; others held them higher, up under the ribcage. She wondered if she was expected to put her arm around Warren Maddock, or Maddox, but it seemed too early in their acquaintance for that. Still, she had kissed him: could "early" or "late" be said to matter any more?

He was still talking. "No, but it's funny: sometimes you meet a girl and it doesn't seem right at all; other times it does. Like, I've only known you for about half an hour, and now we're old friends . . ."

He steered her down a path where there didn't seem to be any lights at all. As they walked he dropped his hand from her shoulder and worked it up under her arm to cradle one breast. His thumb began to stroke her erect, extraordinarily sensitive nipple, which weakened her knees, and her arm went around his back as a matter of course.

". . . A lot of guys just want one thing from a girl, especially after they're in the Army; I don't understand that. I like to get to *know* a girl—get to know her whole personality, you know what I mean? You're nice, Emily; I always have liked skinny girls—I mean *you* know, slender girls . . ."

Only when she felt grass and earth underfoot did she realize they had left the path. He was leading her out across a small meadow, and when they came into near-total darkness under a rustling tree there was nothing awkward about the way they sank to the ground together: it was as smooth as a maneuver on a dance floor, and it seemed dictated by his thumb on her nipple. For a little while they lay writhing together and kissing; then his big hand was moving high up her thigh and he was saying "Oh, let me, Emily, let me . . . It's okay, I've got something . . . Just let me, Emily . . ."

She didn't say yes, but she certainly didn't say no. Everything he did—even when he helped her to free one foot from her underpants—seemed to happen because it was urgently necessary: she was helpless and he was helping her, and nothing else mattered in the world.

She expected pain but there wasn't time to brace herself before it was there—it took her by surprise—and with it there began an insistent pleasure, building to what gave every promise of ecstasy before it dwindled and died. He slipped out of her, sank one knee into the grass beside her leg and rolled away, breathing hard; then he rolled back and took her in his arms. "Oh," he said. "Oh." He smelled pleasantly of fresh sweat and starched cotton.

She felt sore and moist and thought she might be bleeding, but the worst thing was being afraid they would find nothing to talk about. What *did* you talk about, after something like this? When they were back under a park lamp she said "Is my dress dirty?" and after he had put on his overseas cap with great care he fell a step behind her to look.

"Naw, it's fine," he said. "You didn't even get any grass stains. Want to go for a malted or something?"

He took her in a taxi to Times Square, where they drank big chocolate malteds at a stand-up counter and didn't talk at all. Her stomach seemed to constrict on receiving the stuff—she knew she would be sick—but she drank it anyway because it was better than standing there with nothing to say. By the time she'd finished it her nausea was so acute she didn't know if she could make it all the way home before vomiting.

"Ready?" he said, wiping his mouth, and guided her out to the crowded sidewalk by one elbow. "Now you tell me where you live, and we'll see if we can find it on the subway."

Everyone they passed looked grotesque, like figures in a

fever dream: a leering, bespectacled sailor, a drunken Negro in a purple suit, a muttering old woman carrying four greasy shopping bags. There was a wire-mesh municipal trash container on the corner and she ran for it and made it just in time. He came up behind her and tried to hold her arms during the seizure but she shook free of him: she wanted to go through this bleak, humiliating business alone. When the spasms were over, even the dry ones, she found some Kleenex in her purse and cleaned her mouth, but the taste of vomited chocolate malted was still rich in her throat and nose.

"You okay, Emily?" he inquired. "Want me to get you a drink of water?"

"No, that's all right. I'm fine. I'm sorry."

On the downtown IRT local he sat reading the advertisements or inspecting the faces of passengers across the aisle, saying nothing. Even if she'd known how to start a conversation the train was too loud—they would have had to shout—and soon another, more dismal thought occurred to her: now that she'd vomited, he wouldn't want to kiss her goodnight. When they got off the train the fresh air felt good, but their silence continued all the way to Washington Square and to the approximate place in the park where they'd met.

"Where's your home, Emily?"

"Oh, you'd better not take me home. I'll just say good-night here."

"You sure? Will you be okay?"

"Sure. I'm fine."

"Okay, then." And sure enough, all he did was squeeze her arm and give her a little kiss on the cheek. "Take care, now," he said.

Only after turning back to watch him walk away did she

realize how much was wrong: they hadn't exchanged addresses and promises to write; she wasn't even sure of his last name.

"Emmy?" Pookie called from her bed. "How was the movie?"

A week later Pookie answered a ringing telephone at ten o'clock in the morning. ". . . Oh; yes, hello . . . He *what*? Oh my God . . . When? . . . I see . . . God . . . Oh, God . . ." And when she'd hung up the phone she said "Your father died this morning, dear."

"He did?" Emily sat down in a creaking straight chair with her hands in her lap, and she would always remember that on first hearing the news she felt nothing at all.

Pookie said "God" a few more times, as if waiting for it to sink in, and then she began to weep. When her sobs had abated she said "It was pneumonia. He'd been sick for over a week and the doctor was trying to treat him at home, but you know Daddy."

"What do you mean, I 'know' him?"

"I mean *you* know; as long as he was in his own apartment he had his scotch and his cigarettes. Then finally he agreed to go into the hospital yesterday, but it was too late."

"Who called you? The hospital?"

"Mrs. Hammond. *You* know. Irene Hammond, your father's friend."

But Emily didn't know—she'd never heard of Irene Hammond—and now as it occurred to her that Irene Hammond had probably been much more than a friend she began to feel something for the first time. It wasn't grief, exactly; it was more like regret.

"Oh, how I dread calling Sarah," Pookie said. "She's always been her father's baby."

When she did call her, Emily could tell just from hearing Pookie's end of the talk that Sarah's grief was immediate and profound. But if Sarah had always been her father's baby, whose baby was Emily?

At the mortuary they had laid Walter Grimes out to look much younger than his fifty-six years; they'd given him pink cheeks and lips, and Emily didn't want to look at him. But Sarah leaned over and kissed the corpse on the forehead; then Pookie kissed it on the mouth, which made Emily shudder.

Irene Hammond turned out to be a trim, nice-looking woman in her forties. "I've heard *so* much about you girls," she said, and when she shook Tony Wilson's hand she said she'd heard a lot about him too. Then she turned back to Emily and said "I can't tell you how pleased your father was about that scholarship."

The crematory was somewhere in Westchester County, and they rode out there in the limousine following the hearse—Sarah and Tony on the jump seats, Pookie and Emily in back. Behind them came another car carrying Irene Hammond and the few of Walter Grimes's relatives who'd been able to come down from upstate, and then came other cars bringing employees of the New York *Sun*.

There wasn't much of a ceremony at the chapel. An electric organ played, a tired-looking man read a few non-denominational prayers, the casket was removed, and it was over.

"Wait," Sarah said as they filed outside, and she hurried back to her pew and crouched alone to let a last convulsion of sobbing overcome her. It was as if all her mourning in the past few days had not been quite enough—it was required that her bowed face crumple and her shoulders shake one final time.

And Emily had yet to shed a single tear. It troubled her all the way back to the city, and she rode with one hand sandwiched between her cheek and the cool, shuddering glass of the limousine window, as if that might help. She tried whispering "Daddy" to herself, tried closing her eyes and picturing his face, but it didn't work. Then she thought of something that made her throat close up: she might never have been her father's baby, but he had always called her "little rabbit." And she was crying easily now, causing her mother to reach over and squeeze her hand; the only trouble was that she couldn't be sure whether she cried for her father or for Warren Maddock, or Maddox, who was back in South Carolina now being shipped out to a division. But she stopped crying abruptly when she realized that even that was a lie: these tears, as always before in her life, were wholly for herself—for poor, sensitive Emily Grimes whom nobody understood, and who understood nothing.

CHAPTER 4

Sarah gave birth to three sons in three years, and the way Emily could always keep track of their ages was by thinking: Tony Junior was born in my freshman year; Peter in my sophomore year; Eric when I was a junior.

"Oh dear, the way they're *breeding*," Pookie said on hearing of the third pregnancy. "I thought only Italian *peasants* did things like that."

The third pregnancy turned out to be the last—the boys would remain a family of three—but Pookie always managed to suggest, with a rueful little rolling of the eyes, that three was plenty.

Even the news of the first pregnancy had seemed to upset her. "Well, of *course* I'm pleased," she'd told Emily. "It's just that Sarah's so *young*." Pookie had given up the place on Washington Square; she'd found modest employment in a Greenwich Village real estate office and moved into a small walk-up just off Hudson Street. Emily had come down from Barnard to spend a weekend with her, and Pookie was fixing sardine sandwiches for lunch. She pried the last oily shred of sardine from the can with two fingers. "Besides," she said, and sucked the fingers. "Besides, can you imagine me as a grandmother?"

Emily wanted to say I can't even imagine you as a mother, but controlled herself. The important thing on these weekends was to survive them; and tomorrow they were going out to St. Charles, Long Island, for Emily's first pilgrimage to the Wilsons' estate.

"*How* far, did you say?"

"Oh, I forget the exact number of miles," Pookie said, "but it's only a couple of hours on the train. It's really quite a pleasant trip, if you take along something to read."

Emily took along one of her freshman English texts, but she'd scarcely settled down with it before the conductor punched their tickets and said "Change a jamake."

"What did he say?"

"You always have to change at Jamaica for the St. Charles train," Pookie explained. "It doesn't take long."

But it did: they stood for half an hour on the windy Jamaica platform before their train came clattering in, and that was only the beginning of the journey. Were all Long Island trains this loud and dirty and badly in need of repair, or only those going to St. Charles?

When they got off at the tiny station at last Pookie said "There aren't any taxis, of course, because of the war, but it's only a short walk. Aren't the trees beautiful? Smell this fresh air!"

On the short main street of St. Charles they passed a

liquor store and a hardware store and a grubby little store offering BLOOD AND SAND WORMS; then they were on a country road, and the heels of Emily's spectator pumps kept turning under her as she walked. "Is it much farther?" she asked.

"Just beyond this next field. Then we go past a wooded area that's part of the estate, and then we're there. I can't get over how beautiful everything is."

And Emily was willing to acknowledge that the place was nice. Overgrown, but nice. A driveway led off the road into the trees and the high, rustling hedges; where it forked Pookie said "The main house is over there—you can just see a corner of it, but we'll see it later—and Sarah's cottage is this way."

It was a bungalow of white clapboard with a little lawn, and Sarah came out to greet them on the lawn. "Hi," she said. "Welcome to the House at Pooh Corner." She said that as if she'd rehearsed it, and the way she was dressed showed considerable preparation too: bright, fresh maternity clothes that might have been bought for the occasion. She looked lovely.

She served a lunch that was almost as inadequate as one of Pookie's meals; then the problem was that the conversation kept petering out. Sarah wanted to hear "everything" about Barnard, but when Emily began to talk she saw her sister's eyes glaze over in smiling boredom. Pookie said "Isn't this nice? Just the three of us together again?" But it wasn't really very nice at all, and for most of the afternoon they sat around the sparsely furnished living room in attitudes of forced conviviality, Pookie smoking many cigarettes and dropping ashes on the rug, three women with nothing much to say to one another. Color illustrations of Magnum Navy fighter planes in action occupied one wall;

on another was the framed Easter photograph of Sarah and Tony.

Geoffrey Wilson had invited them over to the main house for a drink, and Pookie kept watching the clock: she didn't want to be late.

"You two go ahead," Sarah said. "If Tony gets home in time we'll join you, but he probably won't; he's been putting in a lot of overtime lately."

So they went to the main house without her. It was built of white clapboard too, and it was long and ugly—three stories high in some places and two in others, with black-roofed gables jutting into the trees. The first thing that hit you when you went inside was the smell of mildew. It seeped from the brown oil paintings in the vestibule, from the creaking floor and carpets and walls and gaunt furniture of the long, dark living room.

". . . It's an old house," Geoffrey Wilson was saying as he poured a shot of whiskey for Pookie, "and it's too big to manage without servants, but we try to cope. Will you have scotch too, Emily, or will you join Edna in some sherry?"

"Sherry, please."

"And the worst problem is the heating," he went on. "My father built it as a summer place, you see, and there's never been a proper heating system. One of the tenants did put in an oil burner that looks *vaguely* adequate, but I imagine we'll have to shut off most of the rooms this winter. Well. Cheers."

"*I* think it's a *charming* house," Pookie said, settling down to enjoy the cocktail hour. "I won't hear a word against it. Look, Emmy, see the lovely old portraits? They're some of Geoffrey's ancestors. There are stories connected with every single thing in this room."

"Mostly ve'y dull stories, I'm afraid," Geoffrey Wilson said.

"Fascinating stories," she insisted. "Oh, Geoffrey, I can't tell you how I've come to love it out here—all the lovely meadows and the woodland, and Sarah's cottage, and this wonderful old house. It has such—I don't know; such flair. Does it have a name?"

"A name?"

"You know, the way estates have names. Like 'Jalna,' or 'Green Gables.'"

Geoffrey Wilson pretended to think it over. "The way it looks now," he said, "I suppose we might call it 'Overgrown Hedges.'"

And Pookie didn't realize he was kidding. "Oh, I *like* that," she said. "Not 'Overgrown,' though, that's not quite right. What about"—she worked her lips—"what about 'Great Hedges'?"

"Mm," he said kindly. "Yes; rather nice."

"That's what *I'm* going to call it, anyway," she announced. "'Great Hedges,' St. Charles, Long Island, New York."

"Well." He turned to Emily. "How are you finding your—college?"

"Oh, it's very—interesting." Emily took a sip and sat back to watch her mother get drunk. She knew it wouldn't take long. With the second drink Pookie began to monopolize the talk, telling long pointless anecdotes about houses she'd lived in, hunching forward in her deep chair with her elbows on her slightly parted knees. Emily, sitting across from her, could watch her face loosen as she talked and drank, watch her knees move farther apart until they revealed the gartered tops of her stockings, the shadowed, sagging insides of her naked thighs and finally the crotch of her underpants.

"... No, but the *nicest* house I ever had was in Larchmont. Remember Larchmont, dear? We had real casement windows and a real slate roof; of course we couldn't afford it, but the minute I saw it I said *That's* where I want to live, and I went right in and signed the lease, and the girls loved it. I'll never forget how— Oh, *thank* you, Geoffrey; just one more and then we've really got to be ..."

Why couldn't she get drunk quietly, with her legs curled up in the cushions, like Edna Wilson?

"A little more sherry, Emily?"

"No thanks. I'm fine."

"... And of course the schools were wonderful in Larchmont; that's one reason I wish we could have stayed; still, I've always thought it did the girls a world of good to move around to different places, and then of course ..."

By the time she was ready to leave at last Geoffrey Wilson had to help her to the door. It was getting dark. Emily took her arm—it felt soft and weak—and they made their way past trees and overgrown shrubbery toward the long road to the railroad station. She knew Pookie would sleep on the train—she hoped she would, anyway; it would be better than if she stayed awake and talked—and their dinner, if they had any, would be a hot dog and coffee in Penn Station. But she didn't mind: the weekend was almost over, and in a matter of hours she'd be back in school.

School was the center of her life. She had never heard the word "intellectual" used as a noun before she went to Barnard, and she took it to heart. It was a brave noun, a proud noun, a noun suggesting lifelong dedication to lofty things and a cool disdain for the commonplace. An intellectual might lose her virginity to a soldier in the park, but she could learn to look back on it with wry, amused detachment. An intellectual might have a mother who showed her underpants when drunk, but she wouldn't let it bother her. And Emily Grimes might not be an intellectual yet, but if she took copious notes in even the dullest of her classes, and if she read every night until her eyes ached, it was only a question of time. There were girls in her class, and even a few Columbia boys, who thought of her as an intellectual already, just from the way she talked.

"It's not just a bore," she said once of a tiresome eighteenth-century novel, "it's a *pernicious* bore." And she couldn't help noticing that several other girls made liberal use of the word "pernicious" around the dormitory during the next few days.

But there was more to being an intellectual than a manner of speaking, more even than making the dean's list every semester, or spending all your free time at museums and concerts and the kind of movies called "films." There was learning not to be stricken dumb when you walked into a party full of older, certified intellectuals—and not to make the opposite mistake of talking your head off, saying one inane or outrageous thing after another in a hopeless effort to atone for whatever inane or outrageous thing you'd said two minutes before. And if you did make a fool of yourself at parties like that, you had to learn not to writhe in bed afterwards in an agony of chagrin.

You had to be serious, but—this was the maddening paradox—you had to seem never to take anything very seriously.

"I thought you did very well," said a rumpled man at a party during her sophomore year.

"I what? What do you mean?"

"Just now, when you were talking to Lazlow. I was listening."

"Talking to who?"

"You didn't even know who he is? Clifford Lazlow, political science. He a tiger."

"Oh."

"Anyway, you did very well. You weren't intimidated and you weren't aggressive either."

"But he's just a funny little man in bifocals."

"That's funny." And he shook his plump shoulders to simulate a spasm of laughter. "That's really funny. A funny little man in bifocals. Can I get you a drink?"

"No, actually, I—well, all right."

His name was Andrew Crawford and he was a graduate assistant in philosophy. His damp hair hung in his eyes as he talked, and she wanted to comb it back with her fingers. He wasn't really as pudgy as he'd seemed at first glance; he was attractive in his own way, especially when he was tense with talking, but he looked as though he ought to spend more time outdoors. When he got his doctorate, he said, he would continue to teach—"if the Army doesn't get me, and there's not much chance of that; I'm a physical wreck"—and he would also travel. He wanted to see whatever would be left of Europe, and he wanted to go to Russia too, and China. The world would be made over again in unforeseeable ways, and he didn't want to miss any of it. Essentially, though, he wanted to teach. "I like the classroom," he said. "I know it sounds stuffy, but I like the academic life. What's your field?"

"Well, I'm only a sophomore; I'm an English major, but I don't really—"

"Really? You look older than that. I mean you don't look older, but you *seem* older. The way you move around;

the way you handled old Lazlow. I could've sworn you were a grad student. You have a very—I don't know. You seem very sure of yourself. In a good way, I mean. These parties get a little thick after a while, don't you think? Everybody shouting each other down, everybody trying to score points. It's all ego, ego, ego. You ready for a refill?"

"No; I'd better be going."

"Where do you live? I'll take you home."

"No, actually, I'm with someone."

"Who?"

"You wouldn't know him; Dave Ferguson. He's over there by the door; the tall one."

"Him? But he's only about fifteen years *old*."

"That's silly. He's twenty-one."

"Why isn't he in the Army? Strapping youth like that."

"He has a bad knee."

"A 'trick knee,' right?" Andrew Crawford said. "A 'football knee.' Oh, yes, dear God, I know the type."

"Well, I don't know what you're implying, but I—"

"Not implying anything at all. I never imply. Always say exactly what I mean."

"Anyway, I have to go."

"Wait." And he started after her through the crowd. "Could I call you sometime? Can I have your number?"

As she wrote down the number she wondered why she was doing it. Wouldn't it have been perfectly easy to say no to Andrew Crawford? But that was the trouble: it *wouldn't* have been easy. There was something about him— his eyes, his mouth, his soft-looking shoulders—that suggested he'd be hurt beyond all reason if you said no.

"Thank you," he said, putting her number in his pocket, and he looked as pleased as a child singled out for praise. "Oh, thank you."

"Who was the little fat guy?" Dave Ferguson inquired when they were out on the street.

"I don't know. A graduate student in philosophy. I wouldn't exactly call him fat." After a while she said "Arrogant, though." And then she was troubled again: you couldn't exactly call him arrogant, either.

"He sure had the hots for you."

"You say that about everybody."

It was a clear night, and she enjoyed walking with Dave Ferguson. He held her close but not in the clutching, almost desperate way some boys did; his legs matched her stride perfectly, and their heels made a sharp, invigorating cadence on the street.

"Can I come up?" he asked at her doorstep. She had her own apartment in "approved student housing" now; she had let him "come up" three or four times, and twice he had stayed all night.

"I don't think so tonight, Dave," she said, not quite meeting his eyes. "I'm really very—"

"What's the matter? You sick?"

"No; it's just that I'm so tired I want to go right to sleep. And I've got that awful Chaucer exam tomorrow."

After turning back to watch him retreat up the sidewalk, hunched in his raincoat, she wondered why she had sent him away. Life was confusing.

One distressing thing Emily learned in college was to feel more intelligent than her sister. She had felt more intelligent than her mother for years, but that was different; when it happened with Sarah she felt she had betrayed a trust.

She began to notice it when she and Pookie went out to St. Charles soon after Sarah's second boy was born. Tony

Junior was standing now, drooling and clinging to his mother's leg as they peered into the crib at the small new face.

"Oh, I think Peter's a lovely name," Pookie said. "And you're right, Sarah, he *is* different. He and little Tony have whole different personalities. Don't they, Emmy?"

"Mm."

With the inspection over and the babies asleep, they sat around the living room and Sarah poured three glasses of sherry. She had evidently picked up sherry from Edna Wilson.

"*Oh*, it feels so good to sit down," she said, and she did look tired; but she began to look refreshed as she talked. There were times, especially with a little alcohol in her veins, when Sarah could be almost as much of a talker as Pookie.

"... I couldn't help thinking of Daddy back in August or whenever it was, when Italy surrendered. Did you see the papers that day? The headlines? Well, the *News*—that's the only paper we get; Tony likes it—the *News* headline was 'ITALY QUITS'; but I happened to be down in the village that day so I saw all the other papers. The *Times* and the *Tribune* said 'ITALY SURRENDERS,' or something like that, and so did most of the others. But do you know what the *Sun* said? Daddy's paper? The dear old *Sun*'s headline was 'ITALY CAPITULATES.' Can you imagine? Can you imagine *Daddy* writing a headline like that, or ever allowing it to be written? He would have died. I mean," she added quickly, "he never would've let it happen." And she took a deep drink.

"I don't get it," Emily said.

"Oh, Emmy," Sarah said. "How many people know what 'capitulate' means?"

"Do you know what it means?"

Sarah blinked. "Well, but I mean how many *other* people do? And for a daily newspaper that's supposed to reach millions of people—I don't know; I thought it was funny, that's all."

"Marvelous," Pookie said.

Sarah sat back in the sofa, tucking her ankles up beneath her—had she copied that gesture from Edna Wilson too?—and launched into her next monologue with the zest of a performer who knows her audience will be enthralled. "Oh, I *must* tell you this," she began. "First of all, I got a letter from Donald Clellon last year, and he—"

"Donald Clellon?" Emily said. "Did you really?"

"Oh, just sort of a sad little letter; that's not important. He said he was in the army now and he often thought of me—*you* know—and he said he was out here at Camp Upton. So anyway—"

"How long ago was that?"

"I don't know; a year or so ago. Anyway, last month we had an air-raid scare out here—did you hear about that?"

"Oh, *no*," Pookie said, looking concerned.

"Well, it was nothing, of course, that's the whole point. It only lasted a few hours. *I* wasn't frightened, but some of the little townspeople were—they talked about it for days afterwards. *Any*way, they announced on the radio that one of the soldiers at Camp Upton had turned in the alarm by mistake, and I said—I told this to Tony and he couldn't stop laughing—I said 'I bet it was Donald Clellon.' "

Pookie threw back her head for peal after peal of hearty laughter, showing her bad teeth, and Sarah was helpless with laughter too.

"Well, but wait," Emily said while her mother and sister

were recovering. "Camp Upton is only an induction center; they only stay there a few days before they go to other camps for basic training, and then they're shipped out to divisions. If it was a year ago that Donald wrote you, he's probably overseas by now." And she would have added He might even be dead, but didn't want to overdo it.

"Oh?" Sarah said. "Well, I didn't know that, but even so."

"Oh, Emmy," Pookie said. "Don't spoil the story. Where's your sense of humor?" And she repeated the punch line, to savor it. " 'I bet it was Donald Clellon.' "

Emily didn't know where her sense of humor was, but she knew it wasn't here—nor would it be in the main house, later this afternoon, when she and Pookie went over there for their ritual visit with the elder Wilsons. She guessed she had left it, along with everything else that mattered, back at school.

For a little while she expected Andrew Crawford to call her any day; then she stopped thinking about it, and more than a whole year went by before he did—the year she became a junior.

She had broken off with Dave Ferguson and spent six romantic, melancholy weeks with a boy named Paul Resnick who was waiting to be drafted; he later wrote her a long letter from Fort Sill, Oklahoma, explaining that he loved her but didn't want to be tied down. She worked that summer in an upper-Broadway bookstore—"English majors make good booksellers," the manager told her; "I'll take an English major every time"—and then the following winter, out of the blue, Andrew Crawford called her.

"I wasn't at all certain you'd remember me," he said as they settled into a booth in a Greek restaurant near the Columbia campus.

"Why did you wait so long to call?"

"I was shy," he said, opening his napkin. "I was shy and also I was miserably involved with a young lady whose name shall not be mentioned here."

"Oh. What do people call you, anyway? Andy?"

"Oh, Lord, no. 'Andy' suggests some devilish, hell-for-leather sort of fellow; not my type at all, I'm afraid. I've always been called Andrew. A little hard to get your mouth around, I'll admit—sort of like Ernest or Clarence—but I'm used to it."

From the way he ate she could tell he liked his food—he *was* a little chubby—and he didn't say much until he was full, by which time there was a faint shine of grease around his mouth. Then he began to talk as if talking were another sensual pleasure, using words like "tangential" and "reductive." He talked of the war not as a cataclysm that might soon swallow him up—he said for the second time that he was a physical wreck—but as a complex and fascinating international game; he went on to talk of books she'd never read and authors she'd never heard of, and then he was talking about classical music, of which she knew almost nothing. ". . . And as you may know, the piano part in that sonata is one of the most difficult pieces in the world. Technically, I mean."

"Are you a musician, too?"

"Used to be, sort of. I studied piano and clarinet for many years—you know, I was one of these tiresome little creatures called 'gifted children'—then when it turned out I didn't have the talent to perform I tried composing. Studied composition at Eastman until it was clear I didn't have much talent for that either; then I gave up music altogether."

"It must be very—painful to give up something like that."

"Oh, it broke my heart. But then, back in those days my heart was getting broken on an average of about once a month, so it was only a matter of degree. What would you like for dessert?"

"How often does your heart get broken now?"

"Mm? Oh, somewhat less frequently. Perhaps two or three times a year. What about dessert? They have marvelous baklava here."

She decided she liked him. She didn't much like the grease around his mouth, but he wiped that away before digging into his baklava, and she liked everything else. No other boy she'd known had such a wide general knowledge and so many well-reasoned opinions—he *was* an intellectual —nor had any other boy had the maturity to be self-deprecating. But that was the point: he wasn't a boy. He was thirty. He had come to terms with the world.

She allowed herself to nestle close to his arm as they walked, and when they came to her doorway she said "Would you like to come up for some coffee?"

He backed two steps away on the sidewalk, looking surprised. "No," he said, "no, really; thanks very much; some other time." And he didn't even kiss her; all he did was smile and make an awkward little wave of the hand as he turned away. Upstairs, she walked the floor for a long time with one knuckle in her mouth, trying to figure out what she'd done wrong.

But he did call her again a few days later. This time they went to a Mozart concert, and when they got back to her place he said he thought a little coffee might be pleasant.

He sat on the sofa-bed her mother had helped her buy at the Salvation Army outlet, and as she fussed around the kitchenette she didn't know whether to sit beside him or in the chair across the coffee table. She chose to sit beside him, but he seemed not to notice it. When she leaned back he leaned forward, stirring his coffee, and when she leaned forward he leaned back. All this time he was talking, first about the concert and then about the war and the world and himself.

She reached for a cigarette (she needed something to do with her hands) and she had just lighted it when he made a lunge for her. Sparks flew into her hair and down the front of her dress; she was on her feet, brushing herself off, and he was all apologies. "God, I'm sorry; that was clumsy; I'm always doing things like—you must think I'm—"

"It's all right," she told him. "You startled me, that's all."

"I know; I—I'm terribly sorry."

"No, really; it's all right." She got rid of the cigarette and sat down with him again, and this time his reaching arms went smoothly around her. His face was pink when he kissed her, and she noticed too that he didn't grope for her breasts and her thighs right away, as boys usually did; he seemed to enjoy just hugging and kissing, which he accompanied with soft little moans.

After a while he pulled away from her mouth and said "When's your first class in the morning?"

"Oh, it doesn't matter."

"It does, though. Look at the time. Really, I'd better go."

"No; stay. Please. I want you to stay."

And only then did he begin making love to her. Moaning, he tore off his coat and tie and dropped them on the floor; then he urgently helped her to unfasten her dress. In a few quick, awkward motions she made the sofa into a bed and they were deep inside it, writhing and gasping and clinging together. His warm, heavy torso was soft to the touch, but he was strong.

"Oh," he said. "Oh, Emily, I love you."

"No, no; don't say that."

"But it's true; I have to say it. I love you."

He lay mouthing and sucking one of her nipples for a while, stroking her with his hands; then his mouth went to the other one. After a long time he rolled partly away from her and said "Emily?"

"Yes?"

"I'm sorry, it's—I can't. This happens to me sometimes. I can't."

"Oh."

"I can't tell you how sorry I am; it's just one of those— Does it make you hate me?"

"No, of course not, Andrew."

With a great deflating sigh he heaved himself up and sat on the edge of the bed, and he looked so dejected that she put her arms around him from behind.

"Good," he said. "That's nice. I like to have you hold me that way. And it's true: I do love you. You're delightful. You're sweet and healthy and kind and I love you. It's just that I can't seem to—demonstrate it tonight."

"Sh-sh. It's all right."

"Tell me the truth. Has this ever happened to you before? Has a man ever failed you this way before?"

"Sure."

"You'd say that even if it wasn't true. Ah, God, you're a nice girl. Listen, though, Emily: it's a thing that only happens to me sometimes. Do you believe that?"

"Of course."

"The rest of the time I'm fine. My God, sometimes I can screw and screw until—"

"Sh-sh. It's all right. It was just tonight. There'll be other nights."

"Do you promise? Do you promise me that?"

"Of course."

"That's marvelous," he said, and turned around to take her in his arms.

But for a week, including several afternoons as well as nights and mornings, they tried and tried again without success. Afterwards, what she remembered best about that week was the heat and sweat of their struggle and the smell of the bed.

Several times she said "It must be my fault," and he told her if she talked that way it would only make things worse.

Once he almost accomplished it: he worked his way inside her, and she could feel him. "There!" he said. "Oh, God, there; there—" but it wasn't long before he slipped out and lay heavily on her, panting or sobbing in defeat. "I lost it," he said. "I lost it."

She stroked his damp hair. "It was wonderful for a minute."

"That's kind of you, but I know it wasn't 'wonderful.' It was only the beginning."

"Well, it was the beginning, Andrew. We'll do better next time."

"God. That's what I always say. Every time I leave you and go back into that miserable, brutal, screaming world I think 'I'll do better next time.' And it's always the same —always, always the same."

"Sh-sh. Let's just sleep now. Then maybe in the morning we'll—"

"No. It's even worse in the morning. You know that."

During a warm February thaw he called her to announce he had made a decision. It couldn't be discussed on the phone; could she meet him at the West End at four-thirty?

She found him alone at the bar with a stein of beer, one foot cocked on the rail, and he walked with long strides as he led her to a booth, carrying his shoulders in an easy slouch. That was something she'd noticed before: when she met him somewhere, in a bar or on a street corner, he always moved with the demeanor of an athlete at rest.

He sat close beside her in the booth, holding one of her hands between the beers, and told her he had decided to see a psychoanalyst. He had gotten the man's name from someone "in the department"; he had arranged for his first session and was willing to go as often as necessary—twice, three times a week; he didn't care. It would take all of his savings and much of his salary—he might even have to borrow money—but there was no other way.

"Well, that's—very brave of you, Andrew."

He squeezed her hand. "It's not brave; it's an act of desperation. It's something I probably should have done long ago. And Emily, this is the difficult part: I don't think we ought to see each other while I'm in therapy. Let's say for at least a year. Then I'll look you up again, and of course you'll probably be involved with another man; I can only hope you'll still be free. Because the point is I want to marry you, Emily, and I—"

"You want to *marry* me? But you haven't even—"

"Please," he said, closing his eyes as if in pain. "I know what I haven't even done."

"I wasn't going to say that. I was only going to say you haven't even proposed to me yet."

"You're the sweetest, healthiest, kindest girl I've ever met," he said, and put his arm around her. "Of course I haven't—how could I, under the circumstances? But as soon as this year is over, as soon as I'm—you know—I'll come back and offer you the most heartfelt proposal of marriage you've ever heard. Do you understand, Emily?"

"Well, yes. Except that I—well, yes. Sure, I understand."

"That's marvelous. Now let's get out of here before I burst into tears."

It was a pleasant day—young couples crowded the sidewalk, out to enjoy the false spring—and he led her quickly to a florist's shop on the corner.

"I'm going to put you in a cab and send you home," he said, "but first I'm going to buy you flowers."

"No, that's silly; I don't want any flowers."

"Yes you do. Wait." He came out of the shop with a dozen yellow roses and pressed them into her hands. "Here. Put them in water; then you'll remember me at least until they die. Emily? Will you miss me?"

"Of course."

"Just pretend I've gone off to war, like all the other, better men you've known. All right. No long goodbyes." He kissed her cheek; then he loped into the street, still moving in the athletic way that wasn't natural to him; he flagged down a taxicab and stood there holding the door open for her, smiling with bright eyes that looked a little out of focus.

As the cab pulled away she turned around in the heavy scent of roses to see if he would wave, but she caught only a glimpse of his back heading into the sidewalk crowd.

Except that she wanted to cry, she didn't really know what she felt. She tried to figure it out all the way home until she discovered, climbing the stairs, that she felt a great sense of relief.

Soon after the war ended in Europe, a young merchant seaman came into the bookstore and began talking to her as if he'd known her all her life. His fingernails were broken and black, but he could recite long passages of Milton and Dryden and Pope from memory without seeming to show off: there was, he said, plenty of time for reading aboard ship. He wore a black sweater that looked too warm for the season, and he had a big, blond, handsome head that she described to herself as "Nordic." He stood talking, shifting his weight from one foot to the other, holding a stack of books against his hip, and she felt a powerful urge to put her hands on him. She was afraid he might leave the store without asking her for a date, and he almost did—he said "Well; see you," and started to turn away, but then he turned back and said "Hey, listen: what time do you get off work?"

He was staying in a rundown hotel in Hell's Kitchen—she soon came to know everything about that hotel, from the smells of piss and disinfectant in the lobby to the slow cage of the elevator to the raddled green carpet in his room —and his ship was undergoing extensive repairs in the Brooklyn Navy Yard, which meant he would be in New York all summer. His name was Lars Ericson.

He was as hard and smooth as ivory, and beautifully proportioned; at first she thought she could never get enough of him. She liked to lie in his bed and watch him move naked around the room: he reminded her of Michelangelo's *David*. There were small carbuncular knobs on the back of his neck and out across his shoulders, but if she squinted very slightly she didn't see them.

"... And you've really had no education at all?"

"Of course I have. I've told you; I went through the eighth grade."

"And you really speak four languages?"

"I never told you that. I'm only fluent in French and Spanish. My Italian's very sketchy, very primitive."

"Ah, God, you're wonderful. Come over here ..."

She hoped he might want to be a writer or a painter—she had a vision of him working in a windswept beach cottage, like Eugene O'Neill, while she waded thigh-deep to gather clams and mussels for their supper and the wheeling gulls screamed overhead—but he was perfectly content to be a seaman. He said he liked the freedom it gave him.

"Well, but I mean, freedom to do what?"

"Not necessarily to 'do' anything. Freedom to be."

"Oh. I see. At least I think I see."

She thought she saw a great many things in that voluptuous, invigorating summer with Lars Ericson. She thought she saw that her time in college was a waste. Maybe *anybody's* time in college was a waste. And maybe that had something to do with the tragedy of a man like Andrew Crawford: he had given his life to academia—not just his mind, but his life—and it had shriveled his manhood.

In any case, there was certainly nothing wrong with Lars Ericson's manhood. It grew from him like the sturdy limb of a tree; it prodded and thrusted and plunged in her; it drove her slowly and steadily into a long-sustained delirium for which the only possible expression was a scream; it left her weak and panting and feeling like a woman, waiting for more.

One night as they lay exhausted in his bed there was a knock on the door, and the voice of an adolescent boy called "Lars? You home?"

"I'm home," he called back, "but I'm busy. I have a guest."

"Oh."

"I'll see you tomorrow, Marvin," he said. "Or maybe not tomorrow, but you know; I'll see you around."

"Okay."

"Who was that?" she asked when the footsteps went away.

"Just a kid from the ship. He likes to come in and play

chess sometimes. I feel kind of sorry for him: he's all alone here, doesn't have much to do."

"He ought to get out and find a girl."

"Oh, I think he's too shy for that. He's only seventeen."

"I'll bet *you* weren't too shy at that age. Or no, wait—I'll bet you were shy, but the girls wouldn't leave you alone. Not just girls—older women. Chic, sophisticated older women with penthouses. Right? And they'd get you up in their penthouses and take off all your clothes with their teeth, and they'd run their tongues all over your chest, and they'd go down on their knees and beg for you. Right? Isn't that the way it was?"

"I don't know, Emily. You've got quite an imagination."

"You *kindle* my imagination; you *feed* my imagination. Oh, feed me. Feed me."

One afternoon he showed up at her apartment wearing a cheap new gas-blue suit with padded shoulders—no Columbia boy would be caught dead in a suit like that, but that only added to its charm—and said he'd borrowed a car for the evening. Would she like to drive out to Sheepshead Bay and have a shore dinner?

"That'd be lovely. Who'd you borrow the car from?"

"Oh, a friend. Man I know."

On the long drive through Brooklyn he seemed pre-occupied. He steered with one hand and used the other to play with his mouth, repeatedly pulling out his lower lip and letting it go back against his teeth, and he scarcely talked to her at all. She had hoped they might sit side by side in the restaurant, so he could put his arm around her and they could murmur and laugh together throughout the meal; instead they were across from each other at a big table in the middle of the sawdust-sprinkled floor.

"Is there a place out here," she inquired, "where we could go dancing after dinner?"

"Not that I know of," he said around a mouthful of lobster.

The food rode heavily in her stomach all the way home —there had been too much grease on the fried potatoes —and Lars didn't break his silence until he'd found a parking space near her building. Then, sitting in the stilled car and looking straight through the windshield, he said "Emily, I don't think we ought to see each other any more."

"You don't? Why?"

"Because I have to be true to my own nature. You're very nice and we've had some good times, but I have to think of my own needs."

"I'm not tying you down, Lars. You're as free as—"

"I didn't *say* you were tying me down. I simply said I have to be true to my own—Emily, the point is there's someone else."

"Oh? What's she like?"

"It isn't a girl," he said as if that would make it easier, "it's a man. I happen to be bisexual, you see."

All the moisture went out of her mouth. "You mean homosexual?"

"Of course not; you ought to know better than that. I said *bi*sexual."

"Doesn't that amount to the same thing?"

"No; not at all."

"But you like men better than women."

"I like both. I've enjoyed one kind of experience with you; now I feel I'm ready for the other."

"I see," she said. And when would she ever learn to stop saying "I see" about things she didn't see at all?

He walked her to her door and they stood facing each other on the sidewalk, a few feet apart.

"I'm sorry it has to end this way," he said. He put one hand low on his hip and gazed off down the street in order to let her admire his profile, and he looked more than ever like Michelangelo's *David*, even in that awful suit.

"So long, Lars," she said.

There would be no more sex, she promised herself as she drove her fist repeatedly into the pillow upstairs. She would meet men, she would go out with them and laugh and dance and do all the other things you were supposed to do, but there would be no more sex until—well, until she was absolutely sure of what she was doing.

She broke her promise in November with a haggard law student who said he was a communist, and broke it again in February with a witty boy who played the drums in a jazz combo. The law student stopped calling her because he said she was "ideologically impure," and it turned out that the drummer had three other girls.

Then it was spring again. She was about to graduate from college with no idea of what to do with her life, and it was almost time for Andrew Crawford to end his psychoanalytical exile.

"Emily?" he said on the telephone one evening. "Are you alone?"

"Yes. Hello, Andrew."

"I can't tell you how many times I've started to dial this number and quit on the seventh digit. But you're really there, aren't you. I'm really talking to you. Listen: before I go any further I've got to know this. Are you—do you have a man?"

"No."

"That's almost too good to be—I hardly dared hope for that."

She met him at the West End the following afternoon. "Two beers," he told the waiter. "Or no, wait. Two very dry, extra dry martinis."

He looked about the same—maybe a little heavier; she couldn't be sure—and his face was bright with nervous tension.

". . . Nothing's more boring than hearing about someone else's analysis," he was saying, "so I'll spare you that. Let me just say it's been a tremendous experience. Difficult, painful—God, you can't imagine how painful—but a tremendous experience. It may go on for several more years, but I've turned the first corner. I *feel* so much better. The world isn't filled with terrors for me any more. I feel I know who I am for the first time in my life."

"Well, that's wonderful, Andrew."

He took a greedy sip of his martini and settled back in the booth with a sigh, dropping one hand to her thigh. "And how about you?" he said. "How was your year?"

"Oh, I don't know. All right."

"I vowed I wouldn't ask you this," he said, "but now that I have your marvelous thigh in my hand I've got to know. How many affairs have you had?"

"Three."

He winced. "God. Three. I was afraid you might say eight or ten, but in a way three is worse. Three suggests real, important affairs. It suggests you've been in love with three different men."

"I don't know what love is, Andrew. I've told you that."

"You told me that last year. And you still don't know? Well, good; that's something, anyway. Because you see I *do* know what love is, and I'm going to work on you and work on you until you do too. Oh, listen to me—'work on you.' That sounds as if I meant—God, I'm sorry."

"You don't have to apologize."

"I know. That's what Dr. Goldman keeps telling me. He says I've spent my life apologizing."

There were more martinis at the Greek restaurant, and wine with dinner, and when they started home to her place he seemed a little drunk. She didn't know whether that was a good sign or a bad one.

"This is taking on all the aspects of a major sporting event," he said as they approached her steps. "A championship fight, or something. The contender's been in training for a year; can he make it this time? Stay tuned for Round One, after this word from—"

"Don't, Andrew." She settled her arm around his broad back. "It's not like that at all. We'll just go upstairs and make love to each other."

"Ah, you're so sweet. You're so sweet and healthy and kind."

They tried for hours—they tried everything—and it was no better than the best of their times last year. In the end he sat slumped on the edge of the bed as if on a prizefighter's stool, his head hanging.

"So," he said. "A technical knockout in the fourth round. Or was it only the third? You're the winner and still champion."

"Don't, Andrew."

"Why not? I'm only trying to make light of it. At least the sportswriters will be able to say I was graceful in defeat."

And the following night he scored a victory. It wasn't perfect—in its climactic moments she failed to respond as fully as she knew she should—but it was what the author of any sex manual would have called an adequate performance.

". . . Oh, Emily," he said when he'd recovered his breath, "oh, if only this had happened the first time, last year, instead of all those miserable nights of—"

"Sh-sh." She stroked his shoulder. "That's all in the past now."

"Right," he said. "All in the past. Now let's think about the future."

They were married soon after her graduation, in a civil ceremony at the Municipal Building. The only attendants, or witnesses, were a young married couple of Andrew's acquaintance named Kroll. When they walked out across City Hall Park afterwards for what Mrs. Kroll insisted on calling "the wedding breakfast," Emily found herself in one of the busy lunchtime restaurants she had come to with her father long ago.

They told their mothers first. Pookie wept into the telephone, as Emily had known she would, and made them promise to come and visit her the next night. Andrew's mother, who lived in Englewood, New Jersey, invited them for the following Sunday.

". . . Oh, he's nice, dear," Pookie said when she'd cornered Emily in the cramped kitchen downtown, while Andrew sat sipping coffee in the next room. "I was a little—well, frightened of him at first, but when you get to know him he's really awfully nice. And I love the sort of formal way he talks; he must be *very* intelligent . . ."

Andrew's mother was older than Emily had expected, a blue-haired, wrinkled and powdered woman wearing knee-length elastic stockings. She sat on a chintz-covered sofa with three white Persian cats, in a room that smelled of recent vacuum cleaning, and she blinked at Emily repeatedly as if having to remind herself that Emily was there. In a bright, airless sun porch called "the music room" there was an upright piano, and there was a framed studio photograph of Andrew at the age of eight or nine, dressed in a sailor suit, seated on the piano bench with a clarinet across his chubby lap. Mrs. Crawford opened the keyboard and looked imploringly at her son. "Play something for us, Andrew," she said. "Has Emily heard you play?"

"Oh, Mother, please. You know I don't play any more."

"You play like an angel. Sometimes when there's Mozart or Chopin on the radio I just close my eyes"—she closed her eyes—"and picture you here—right here at this piano . . ."

In the end he gave in: he played a short selection from Chopin, and even Emily could tell he was hurrying through it, seeming to play sloppily on purpose.

"God!" he said when they were back on the train for New York. "Every time I go out there it takes me days to recover —whole days just to get to the point where I can *breathe* again . . ."

Only one visit remained to be made—to Sarah and Tony in St. Charles—and they put it off until the end of the summer, when Andrew had bought a used car.

"So," he said as they sped along the wide Long Island highway. "At last I get to meet your beautiful sister and your dashing, romantic brother-in-law. I feel as if I'd known them for years."

He was in a sour, touchy mood, and she knew why. His sexual performance had been adequate all summer, with occasional lapses, but just lately—in the past week or so

—he had fallen back into the old habit of failure. Last night he had suffered a premature ejaculation against her leg, and afterwards he had wept in her arms.

"Was he in the service?"

"Who?"

"Laurence Olivier. Who'd you think I meant?"

"I've told you," she said. "He was drafted into the Navy, but they assigned him back to Magnum as naval personnel."

"Well, at least he didn't storm the beaches at Normandy," Andrew said, "and win the Silver Star with fourteen Oakleaf Clusters—we'll be spared *that* kind of an evening."

It wasn't easy to find St. Charles from the spidery lines on the road map, but once they were in the village she saw enough landmarks (BLOOD AND SAND WORMS) to guide Andrew out to the Wilsons' place. Beside the driveway was a small hand-lettered sign reading GREAT HEDGES, and she recognized the lettering as Sarah's.

The young Wilsons sat on a blanket on their front lawn with their three sons toddling and chirping around them in the afternoon sunshine; they were so absorbed in each other that they didn't see their guests arrive.

"I wish I had a camera," Emily called. "You make a lovely picture."

"Emmy!" Sarah sprang to her feet and came forward across the bright grass with both arms held out. "And you're Andrew Crawford—it's *so* nice to meet you."

Tony's greeting was less effusive—his smiling eyes, crinkled at the corners, seemed more amused than pleased, as if he were thinking Must I really put myself out for this fellow? Just because he's married to my wife's little sister? —but he shook Andrew's hand firmly enough and managed to mumble appropriate things.

"I didn't know even *Eric* was on his feet now," Emily said.

"Certainly," Sarah told her. "He's almost eighteen months old. And that's Peter there, the one with the cookie crumbs on his face, and the big one's Tony Junior. He's three and a half. What do you think of them?"

"They're beautiful, Sarah."

"We just came out here to get the last of the sun," Sarah said, "but let's go inside. It's cocktail time. Darling? Would you shake out the blanket, please? It's all cookie crumbs."

Cocktail time, in the carefully cleaned-up living room, meant that the Crawfords had to sit and watch with fixed smiles while the Wilsons went through the old Anatole's business of entwining arms for the first sip. For what seemed a long time after that the party failed to ignite. Shadows lengthened on the floor and the west windows turned bright gold, and still the four of them were stiff and shy. Even Sarah was less talkative than usual: she told no rambling anecdotes, and except for a few awkwardly phrased questions about Andrew's work she seemed constrained in his presence, as if afraid she might appear trivial to such a learned man.

"Philosophy," Tony said, swirling the ice cubes in his empty glass. "I'm afraid that whole field's rather a mystery to me. Must be ve'y difficult to read, let alone teach. How does one go about teaching it?"

"Oh, well," Andrew said, "you know; we get up there and try to educate the little bastards."

Tony chuckled approvingly, and Sarah turned her laughing face on him as if to say You see? You see? I *told* you Emmy wouldn't marry a creep.

"I say, are we ever going to eat?" Tony inquired.

"I'll have just one more cigarette," Sarah said. "Then I'll get the boys to bed, and then we'll have dinner."

The small roast was badly overcooked and so were the vegetables, but Andrew had been warned not to expect very much in the way of food. It began to seem that the visit might be a success after all, for all of them, until they moved back into the living room after coffee.

There were more drinks then, in taller glasses, and the trouble might have been partly that: Andrew wasn't used to drinking that much, and he grew a little over-earnest in recommending a Jugoslavian movie, or "film," that he and Emily had seen. ". . . I don't see how anyone could fail to be moved by it," he concluded, "anyone with any belief in humanity."

Tony had looked sleepy through most of the recital, but the last line brought him awake. "Oh, I believe in humanity," he said. "Humanity's perf'ly all right with me." Then his mouth went into a subtle shape of wit, suggesting that his next remark would bring down the house. "I like everyone but coons, kikes, and Catholics."

Sarah had started to laugh in anticipation of whatever he might say, but when she heard it she cut her laughter short and lowered her eyes, displaying the fine little blue-white scar of the gymnastics bar long ago. There was an uneasy silence.

"Is that something you learned in your English public school?" Andrew inquired.

"Mm?"

"I said is that something they taught you in your English public school? How to say something like that?"

Tony blinked in bewilderment; then he mumbled something inaudible—it might have been "Oh, I say" or "Sorry" or it might have been neither—and stared at his glass with a jaded little smile to show that he for one had had quite enough of this tiresome nonsense.

Somehow a measure of decorum was restored. They managed to labor through a ceremony of small talk and smiles and goodnights, and then they were free.

"The Country Squire," Andrew said, gripping the steering wheel tight in both hands as they droned along the highway toward home. "He was raised with the English upper-middle class. He's 'practically an engineer.' He lives in a place called Great Hedges. He's sired three sons out of his beautiful wife; and he comes up with a remark like that. He's a Neanderthal. He's a pig."

"It was inexcusable," Emily said. "Wholly inexcusable."

"Oh, and by the way, it's true what you told me," Andrew went on, "they *do* read nothing but the *Daily News*. When I went out to the bathroom I passed a stack of *Daily News*es about three feet high—the only bona-fide reading matter in that whole lovey-dovey little house."

"I know."

"Ah, but you love him, don't you?"

"What? What do you mean? I don't 'love' him."

"You've told me," Andrew said. "You can't take it back now. You've told me that when they were first engaged you had fantasies about him. You had fantasies that you were the one he really loved."

"Oh, come on, Andrew."

"And I can imagine what you did to support those fantasies—to flesh them out, so to speak. I'll bet you masturbated over him. Didn't you? Oh, I'll bet you tickled your little nipples until they came up hard, and then you—"

"Stop it, Andrew."

"—and then you went to work on your clitoris—picturing him all the time, imagining what he'd say and how he'd feel and what he'd do to you—and then you spread your legs and shoved a couple of fingers up your—"

"I want you to *stop* this, Andrew. If you don't stop it I'll open this door and get out of this car and—"

"All *right*."

She thought his rage would make him drive too fast, but he was carefully holding the car under the speed limit. His profile, in the dim blue light of the dashboard, was clenched in the look of a man controlling himself against impossible odds. She turned away from him and stared out the window for a long time, watching the slow movement of endless dark, flat land and the red throbbing of radio-tower lights high in the distance. Did women ever divorce their husbands after less than a year of marriage?

He didn't speak again until after they'd crossed the Queensboro Bridge, until after they'd crawled through traffic to the West Side and turned uptown, heading home. Then he said "Do you want to know something, Emily? I hate your body. Oh, I suppose I love it too, at least God knows I try to, but at the same time I hate it. I hate what it put me through last year—what it's putting me through now. I hate your sensitive little tits. I hate your ass and your hips, the way they move and turn; I hate your thighs, the way they open up. I hate your waist and your belly and your great hairy mound and your clitoris and your whole slippery cunt. I'll repeat this exact statement to Dr. Goldman tomorrow and he'll ask me why I said it, and I'll say 'Because I *had* to say it.' So do you see, Emily? Do you understand? I'm saying this because I *have* to say it. I hate your body." His cheeks were quivering. "I hate your body."

PART TWO

CHAPTER
1

For a few years after she divorced Andrew Crawford, Emily worked as a librarian in a Wall Street brokerage house. Then she got another job: she joined the editorial staff of a biweekly trade journal called *Food Field Observer*. It was pleasant, undemanding work, writing news and feature stories for the grocery industry; sometimes when she composed a headline quickly and well, so that the spaces counted out right the first time—

'HOTEL BAR' BUTTER
HITS SALES PEAK;
MARGARINES FADE

—she would think of her father. There was always a dim chance that the job could lead to employment on a real magazine, which might be fun; besides, college had taught her that the purpose of a liberal-arts education was not to train but to free the mind. It didn't matter what you did for a living; the important thing was the kind of person you were.

And most of the time she thought of herself as a responsible, well-rounded person. She lived in Chelsea now, in a place with tall windows facing a quiet street. It could easily have been made into an "interesting" apartment, if she'd cared enough to bother about such things; in any case it was big enough to give parties in, and she liked parties. It also made a snug little temporary home for two, and during that time there were a good many men.

In the space of two years she had two abortions. The first would have been the child of a man she didn't like very much, and the central problem with the second was that she couldn't be sure whose child it would have been. After that second abortion she stayed home from the office for a week, lying around the apartment alone or taking hesitant, painful walks along the empty streets. She thought of going to a psychiatrist—some of the people she knew went to psychiatrists—but it would cost too much and might not be worth the effort. Besides, she had a healthier idea. On a low, sturdy table in her apartment she set up the portable typewriter her father had given her as a high school graduation present and began work on a magazine article.

ABORTION: A WOMAN'S VIEW

She liked the tentative title, but couldn't settle on an opening sentence, or what she had learned to call a "lead."

> It is painful, dangerous, "immoral" and illegal, yet every year more than _____ million women get abortions in America.

That had a nice ring to it, but it set her up for a kind of hortatory stance she would somehow have to maintain throughout the article.

She tried another attack.

> Like many girls of my age, I had always assumed that abortion is a dreadful thing—to be approached, if at all, with the fear and trembling one reserves for a descent into the outer circles of hell.

That sounded better, but even after she'd changed "girls" to "women" it failed to please her. Something was wrong.

She decided to skip the lead for now and plunge into the body of the article. For many hours she wrote many paragraphs, smoking many cigarettes that she was unaware either of lighting or of putting out. Then she went over it with a pencil, scribbling revisions in the margins and sometimes on whole new pages ("Rev. A, pgh. 3, p. 7"), feeling a heady sense of having found her vocation. But the messy stack of manuscript was there waiting for her in the morning, after a fitful sleep; and she had to acknowledge, with an editor's gelid eye, that it didn't read well at all.

When her week of sick leave was over she went back to the office, grateful for the orderly rhythm of an eight-hour day. For several evenings and most of one weekend she worked on the abortion article, but in the end she stowed it in a cardboard box that she called "my files," and put the typewriter away. She would need the table for parties.

Then suddenly it was 1955, and she was thirty years old.

". . . And of course if you want to be a career girl that's fine," her mother said on one of the rare and dreaded evenings when Emily went down to her place for dinner. "I only wish *I'd* found a satisfying career when I was your age. It's just that I do feel—"

"It's not a 'career'; it's only a job."

"Well, all the more reason, then. It's just that I do feel it's time for you to—oh, I won't say 'settle down'; Lord knows *I* never settled down; I just mean—"

"Get married again. Have children."

"Well, is that so strange? Don't you know *any* young man you'd like to marry? Sarah told me she and Tony *loved* the last man you brought out there; what was his name? Fred something?"

"Fred Stanley." He had come to bore her beyond endurance after a few months; she had taken him to St. Charles only on a whim, because he was so presentable.

"Oh, I know, I know," Pookie said with a world-weary smile, digging into her cool spaghetti; she had a full set of false teeth now, which greatly improved her smile. "It's none of my business." Her business came up later that night, after she'd had too much to drink: it was a grievance Emily had heard many times before. "Do you know it's been more than six *months* since I was out at St. Charles? Sarah never invites me. Never invites me. And she *knows* how I love it out there, how I love to spend time with the children. I call up every Sunday and she says 'Well, I guess you'd like to talk to the boys now,' and of course I *love* talking to them, hearing their voices—especially Peter, he's my favorite— and then when we're finished she comes back on and says 'This is costing you a fortune, Pookie, we'd better think about your phone bill.' And I say 'Never *mind* the phone bill, I want to talk to *you*,' but she never invites me. And the few times, the very few times I've suggested it myself she says 'I'm afraid next weekend wouldn't be convenient, Pookie.' Ha. 'Convenient' . . ."

There was a dribble of spaghetti sauce on her mother's

chin, and Emily had to fight an impulse to get up and wipe it off.

"... And when I *think*; when I *think* of the weeks and weeks I spent out there when Tony was gone in the Navy and all three of those babies were in diapers, how I cooked and scrubbed and the furnace didn't work half the time or the pump either, and we had to carry water from the main house—did anyone ever ask if that was 'convenient' for *me*?" To emphasize her point she shook the long ash of her cigarette defiantly on the floor and took another drink of her cloudy, fingerprinted highball. "Oh, I suppose I could always call Geoffrey; *he* understands. He and Edna'd probably invite me, but still—"

"Why don't you?" Emily said, inspecting her watch. "Call Geoffrey, and maybe he'll ask you out for a weekend."

"Ah, well, you're looking at your watch. All right. All right. I know. You have to get back to your job and your parties and your men and whatever else it is you do. I know. Go ahead." And Pookie waved her moist cigarette in dismissal. "Go ahead," she said. "Go ahead; run along."

The following spring the job of managing editor on *Food Field Observer* fell vacant, and for a few days Emily thought she might be promoted, but instead they hired a man of about forty named Jack Flanders. He was very tall and spare with a sad, sensitive face, and Emily found she couldn't keep her eyes off him. His office was separated from hers by a glass partition: she could watch him frown over his pencil or his typewriter, watch him talk on his telephone, watch him get up and stand gazing out his window as if lost in thought (and he couldn't have been thinking about the job). He reminded her a little of her father, long ago. Once when he was on the phone she saw his long face break into a smile of such pure delight that he could only have been talking to a woman, and she felt an irrational twinge of jealousy.

He had a deep, resonant voice, and he was very courteous. He always said "Thanks, Emily," or "That's fine, Emily" when she brought him something in the line of duty, and once he said "That's a pretty dress," but he never seemed to meet her eyes.

On the day of a deadline, when everyone was tired and overworked, she opened a manila envelope to find six glossy photographs, each of what looked like a shallow box or tray made of porous white cardboard. Each box was of different proportions and each picture taken from a different angle, with different lighting, to emphasize a separate aspect of its design. The press release that came with them was breathless with phrases like "revolutionary concept" and "bold new approach," but she distilled from it the information that this was how fresh cuts of meat might now be packaged for sale in supermarkets. She wrote a story long enough to fill half a column, with a two-column head; then she marked up four of the pictures for single-column cuts, wrote short captions for them and took the finished job to Jack Flanders.

"Why so many pictures?" he inquired.

"They sent six; I only used four."

"Mm," he said, frowning. "Wonder why they didn't put any meat in 'em? Couple of pork chops or something. Or show a guy's hand holding the box, so you'd get an idea of the size."

"Mm."

He scrutinized the four photographs for a long time. Then he said "You know something, Emily?" And he looked at her with the beginnings of the same smile she'd seen him submit to on the phone that other day. "There are times when a word—one word—is worth a thousand pictures."

Remembering it later she was able to agree with him that it hadn't really been all that funny, but at the time—and maybe it was just the way he said it—her laughter was overwhelming. She couldn't stop; she was weak; she had to lean against his desk for support. When it was over she found him looking at her with a shy, happy face.

"Emily?" he said. "Think you might come out for a drink with me after work tonight?"

He had been divorced for six years. He had two children who lived with their mother, and he wrote poetry.

"Published?" she asked.

"Three times."

"In magazines, you mean?"

"No, no; books. Three books."

He lived in one of the drab blocks of the West Twenties, just off Fifth Avenue, where random residential buildings are pressed in among the lofts, and his apartment was what she guessed could be called Spartan—no rug, no curtains, no television.

After their fine first night together, when it seemed abundantly clear that this particular long, skinny man was exactly the kind she had always wanted, she prowled along his bookshelves, wearing his bathrobe, until she came to three slim volumes with the name John Flanders on their spines. He was out in the kitchen making coffee.

"My God, Jack," she called. "You were a Yale Younger Poet."

"Yeah, well, it's kind of a lottery," he said. "They have to give it to somebody every year." But his self-effacement didn't quite ring true: she could tell how pleased he was that she'd found the book—he almost certainly would have showed it to her if she hadn't.

She turned it over and read one of the endorsements aloud: " 'In John Flanders we have an authentic new voice, rich in wisdom, passion, and perfect technical control. Let us rejoice in his gift.' Wow."

"Yeah," he said in the same proud-bashful way. "Big deal, huh? You can take that home with you, if you'd like. Fact, I'd like you to. The second book's okay too; probably not as good as the first. Only for Christ's sake don't mess with the third one. It's lousy. You wouldn't believe how lousy. Sugar and milk?"

While they sat sipping coffee, looking out at the tan-and-green loft buildings, she said "What are you doing on a *trade* paper?"

"Got to have some kind of a job. And the point is it's easy; I can do it with my left hand and forget it when I come home."

"Don't poets usually work in universities?"

"Ah, I've had that. Did it for more years than I can count. Kissing ass with the department chairman, sweating out tenure, fending off hordes of solemn, dense little faces all day and having them haunt you all night—and the worst part is you end up writing academic *poetry*. No, baby, believe me, *Food Field Observer* is a better deal."

"Why don't you apply for a whaddyacallit? A Guggenheim?"

"Had it. Had the Rockefeller, too."

"Can you tell me why the third book is lousy?"

"Ah, my whole life was a mess then. I'd just been divorced, I was drinking too much; guess I thought I knew what I was doing in those poems, but I didn't know my ass from third base. Sentimental, self-indulgent, self-pitying— miserable stuff. The last time I saw Dudley Fitts he barely nodded to me."

"And how's your life now?"

"Oh, still pretty much of a mess, I guess, except I've found that sometimes"—he worked his hand up inside the sleeve of the bathrobe to her elbow, which he fondled as if it were an erogenous zone—"sometimes, if you play your cards right, you get to meet a nice girl."

For a week they were never apart—they spent the nights either at his place or at hers—and she never had enough solitude to read his first book, until she took a day off from work for that purpose.

It wasn't easy. She had read a lot of contemporary poetry at Barnard and always done well enough in her "explications," but she never read it for pleasure. She went through the early poems too quickly, getting only impressions of their ideas; then she had to go back and study each one to appreciate how it was made. The later poems were richer, though they retained the quality of seeming to have been spoken in Jack's voice, and almost the whole of the final section of the book was devoted to a single long poem, so intricate and containing what she guessed were so many levels of meaning that she had to read it three times. It was almost five o'clock before she was able to call him at the office and say she thought the book was great.

"Honest to God?" She could almost see the delight in his face. "You wouldn't bullshit me, would you, Emily? Which ones you like best?"

"Oh, I liked them all, Jack. Really. Let me think. I loved the one called 'A Celebration'; it almost made me cry."

"Oh?" He sounded disappointed. "Well, yeah, that's a pleasant little formal lyric, but it hasn't got much meat on its bones. What about the war poem, the one called 'Hand Grenade'?"

"Oh, yes, that one too. It has a nice—acidity to it."

"Acidity; good word. That's exactly what it was supposed to have. And of course I guess the only important question is what did you think of the last one. The big one."

"I was coming to that. It's beautiful, Jack. It's very, very moving. Hurry and come home."

Early in the summer he was invited to teach for two years in the Writers' Workshop at the State University of Iowa.

"You know something, baby?" he said when they'd both read the letter. "Might be kind of a mistake to turn this down."

"I thought you hated teaching."

"Well, but Iowa's different. The way I understand it, this 'Workshop' is wholly separate from the English department. It's a graduate program, kind of a professional school. The kids are carefully chosen—they're not really students at all, they're young writers—and the only 'teaching' I'd have to do would be four or five hours a week. Because the idea is, see, the teachers are supposed to produce their own stuff while they're out there, so they give you plenty of time. And I mean Christ, if I can't get this book wrapped up in two years there's something *really* the matter with me. Besides," he said, shyly rubbing his chin with his thumb, and she could tell that this next consideration would be the clincher of his argument. "Besides—oh, I know this sounds dumb, but it's kind of an honor to be invited out there. Must mean *somebody* doesn't think my last book sank me forever."

"Well, all right, Jack, but the honor's still there whether

you accept the invitation or not. So think about it: do you really want to go to *Iowa*?"

They were both on their feet and pacing the floor of his apartment, as they'd been doing since he opened the letter. He walked over to her across the bare boards, put his arms around her and bent down to hide his face against her hair. "I do want to go," he said, "but I'll only go on one condition."

"What's that?"

"If you come with me," he said huskily, "and stay with me, and be my girl."

In August they both quit their jobs on *Food Field Observer*, and on the last weekend before they left for Iowa she took him out to St. Charles.

"... Oh, I *like* him," Sarah said when she and Emily were alone in the sun-shot kitchen. "I really like him a lot—and Tony does too, I can tell." She paused to lick a fragment of liver paste from her finger. "You know what *I* think you ought to do?"

"What?"

"Marry him."

"What do you mean, 'marry' him? You're always telling me to 'marry' people, Sarah. You say that about every man I bring *out* here. Is marriage supposed to be the answer to everything?"

Sarah looked hurt. "It's the answer to an awful lot of things."

And Emily almost said How would *you* know? but caught herself in time. Instead she said "Well, we'll see," and they carried plates of sloppily made hors d'oeuvres back into the living room.

"Well, of course, my war was a pretty dismal business," Jack was saying, "crawling around Guam with a radio on my back, but I do remember those sleek little Magnum Navy fighters. I used to wonder what it must be like to be up there in one of them, tooling around."

"You ought to see the ones we're turning out now," Tony said. "Jet fighters. Strap yourself into one of those jobs and *Shoom!*" He made a kind of salute, knifing the upright flat of his hand straight ahead from his temple to suggest the speed of the takeoff.

"Yeah," Jack said. "Yeah, I can imagine."

When the boys came in, out of breath, Emily tried not to be too effusive about how much they'd grown since her last visit, but the changes were remarkable. Tony Junior was fourteen now and big for his age, already built like his father. He was a nice-looking kid but there was something a little vacant about his smile, admitting at least the possibility that he might grow up to be an amiable fool; and Eric, the youngest, had developed a guarded look that was more sullen than shy. Only Peter, the middle one, the one Pookie always called her favorite, held her attention. He was thin and tense as a whippet; he had his mother's large brown eyes, and he looked intelligent even while chewing bubble gum.

"Hey, Aunt Emmy?" he said around his chewing. "Remember the Presidents you gave me when I was ten?"

"The present? What present?"

"No, the Presidents."

And finally she did remember. Every Christmas she spent too many hours buying stuff for the boys; she would wade grudgingly through department stores on sore feet, breathing stale air and quarreling with exhausted clerks, and one year she had settled on what she could only hope was a suitable gift for Peter: a flat cardboard box containing white plastic statuettes of every American President through Eisenhower. "Oh, the *Presidents*," she said.

"Right. Anyway, I really enjoyed them."

"Oh, *did* he," Sarah said. "You know what he did? He made this big excavation out in the yard, like a park, with lawns and groves of trees and a river running through it, and bridges over the river, and he set up all the Presidents in different places, each with a different sized pedestal according to his reputation. He gave Lincoln the highest pedestal because he was the greatest, and he put the ones like Franklin Pierce and Millard Fillmore very low—oh, and he gave William Howard Taft a very wide pedestal because he was the fattest, and he—"

"Okay, Mom," Peter said.

"No, but really," she went on. "I wish you could've seen it. And you know what he did with Truman? At first he couldn't decide what to do with Truman, and then he—"

"I think you've about covered it, dear," Tony said with a barely perceptible wink at their guests.

"Oh," she said. "Well, all right." And she quickly took a drink to hide her mouth. That mannerism had never changed: whenever Sarah was embarrassed, after she'd told a joke and was waiting for the laughter, or when she was afraid she'd talked too much, she would go for her mouth as if to cover nakedness—with Cokes or popsicles as a child, with drinks or cigarettes now. Maybe all the years of splayed, protruding teeth, and then of braces, had made her mouth the most vulnerable part of her for life.

Later that afternoon the boys began wrestling on the floor until they knocked over a small table, and their father said "All right, men. Shape up." It was his standard, all-purpose admonition for them; evidently it was something he'd learned in the Navy.

"There's nothing for them to *do* in here, Tony," Sarah said.

"Let them go back outside, then."

"No," she said, "I've got a better idea." And she turned to Emily. "This is something you've *got* to see. Peter? Get the guitars."

Eric folded his arms across his chest to show he didn't mind being left out, and the older boys clambered into another room and came back with two cheap guitars. When they were sure their audience was ready they stood in the middle of the floor, filling the small house with sound, and gave an impersonation of the Everly Brothers:

> *Bye bye, love*
> *Bye bye, happiness...*

Tony Junior was only hitting a couple of simple chords and chanting the words; Peter did all the difficult fingerwork, and he seemed to be putting his heart into the song.

"They're great kids, Sarah," Emily said when they'd gone outside again. "That Peter's really something."

"Have I told you what he wants to be when he grows up?"

"What—President?"

"No," Sarah said, as if that might be one of several viable alternatives. "No, you'd never guess. He wants to be an Episcopalian priest. I took them to the Easter service at the little church here in town a few years ago, and Peter never got over it. Now he gets me up to take him to church every Sunday, or else he hitch-hikes in."

"Oh, well," Emily said, "I imagine that's something he'll probably outgrow."

"Not if I know Peter."

At the dinner table, exhilarated by his afternoon of show-ing off, Peter interrupted the adults with so many silly re-marks that Tony told him to shape up twice. The third time, when he put his napkin on his head, Sarah assumed command. "Peter," she said. "Shape up." She glanced quickly at Tony to see if she'd said it right, then at Emily to see if it had sounded funny, and then she hid her mouth in her glass.

"I understand you're on the radio," Jack Flanders said to Sarah later that evening, when the adults were alone in the living room.

"Oh, not any more," she said, looking pleased. "That's all over now." In the early fifties she had served as "hostess" for a Saturday morning housewives' program on the local Suffolk County radio station—Emily had heard it once, and thought she did very well—but the program had ex-pired after eighteen months. "It was only a little local sta-tion," Sarah explained, "but I did enjoy it—especially writing the scripts. I love to write."

And that led her into a subject she had clearly wanted to bring up for hours: she was writing a book. One of Geoffrey Wilson's ancestors on his mother's side, a New York man named George Fall, had been a Western pioneer. Together with a small group of other Easterners he had helped to clear and settle part of what was now Montana. Little was known about George Fall, but he had written many letters home during his adventures, and one of his nephews had transcribed them into the form of a pamphlet, privately printed, a copy of which had come into Geoffrey Wilson's possession.

"It's fascinating stuff," Sarah said. "Of course, it's pretty hard to read—it's all in this very quaint, old-fashioned style, and you have to use your imagination to fill in the gaps—but the material's all there. I figured *some*body's got to do a book on this; it might as well be me."

"Well, that's—quite an undertaking, Sarah," Emily said, and Jack said it certainly did sound interesting.

Oh, the project was still in the very early stages, she assured them, as if to minimize their envy; she had made a rough outline, finished the Introduction and done a first draft of the opening chapter, but the chapter still needed work. She didn't even have a title yet, though she was thinking of calling it *George Fall's America*, and she would have to do a lot of library research on the period as she went along. The book would take time, but she loved doing it— and it was a wonderful feeling just to be *doing* something again.

"Mm," Emily said. "I can imagine."

"Might even be a little money in it," Tony said, chuckling. "*That*'d cert'ly be a wonderful feeling."

Sarah looked shy, and then suddenly bold. "Would you like to hear my Introduction?" she asked. "It isn't often I have an audience of two real writers. Darling?" she said to her husband. "Why don't you fix us all another drink, and then I'll read my Introduction."

With her shoes off and her ankles snug beneath her buttocks, holding her trembling manuscript high in one hand and allowing her voice to fill out to the timbre appropriate for a small lecture hall, Sarah began to read aloud.

The Introduction told of how George Fall's letters had been preserved, and of how they had provided the basis for this book. There followed a brief summary of his travels that included many dates and place-names, and even that was easy to listen to: Emily was surprised at how well the sentences flowed; but then, Sarah's radio script had surprised her too.

Tony looked sleepy during the reading—he had probably heard it before—and his tolerant downcast smile, as he stared at his drink, seemed to say that if this sort of thing gave the little woman pleasure, well and good.

Sarah had reached her conclusion:

> "George Fall was in many ways a noble man, but he was not unique. In his time there were countless others like him—men who dared, who gave up comfort and security to confront a wilderness, to face adversity against seemingly hopeless odds, to conquer a continent. In a very real sense, then, the story of George Fall is the story of America."

She put the manuscript down, looking shy again, and took a deep drink of whiskey and water.

"That's excellent, Sarah," Emily said. "Really excellent." And Jack said something polite to show he was in total agreement.

"Well, it probably needs work," Sarah said, "but that's the general idea."

". . . Your sister's very sweet," Jack Flanders said when he and Emily were on the train going home. "And she *does* write well; I wasn't just saying that."

"I wasn't just saying it either. I know she does. I can't get over how soft and dumpy she's getting, though. She used to have the most beautiful figure I've ever seen."

"Yeah, well, that happens to a lot of full-blown women," he said. "That's why I like 'em skinny. No, but I see what you mean about your brother-in-law; he *is* kind of a boor."

"I always get the most terrible *headaches* when I go out there," Emily said. "I don't know why, but it never fails. Could you sort of rub the back of my neck?"

CHAPTER 2

Iowa City was a pleasant town, built in the shadow of the university along a slow river. Some of the straight, tree-lined, sun-splashed residential streets reminded Emily of illustrations in *The Saturday Evening Post*—was this what America really did look like?—and she wanted to live in one of their ample old white houses; but then they discovered a small, odd-looking stone bungalow on a dirt road in the country, four miles out of town. It had been built as an artist's studio, the real estate lady explained; that accounted for the outsized living room and the tall picture window. "It wouldn't be at all practical for people with children," she said, "but for just the two of you it might be fun."

They bought a cheap used car and spent several evenings exploring the countryside, which turned out to be far less monotonous than they'd expected. "I thought it'd be all cornfields and prairies," Emily said, "didn't you? And here are all these rolling hills and woods—oh, and doesn't the air smell wonderful?"

"Mm. Yeah."

And it was always a pleasure to come home to the little house.

Soon there was a staff meeting from which Jack returned in an exultant mood. "I don't mean to depart from my customary boyish modesty, baby," he said, pacing the floor with a drink in his hand, "but I happen to be the best poet they've got out here. Maybe the *only* one. Jesus, you ought to meet these other clowns—you ought to *read* them."

She didn't read them, but she met them, at several raucous and confusing parties.

"I liked the older man," she told Jack as they drove home one night. "What's his name? Hugh Jarvis?"

"Yeah, well, Jarvis is okay, I guess. He wrote some good stuff twenty years ago, but he's washed up now. What'd you think of that little bastard Krueger?"

"He seemed very shy. I liked his wife, though; she's—interesting. She's somebody I'd like to get to know."

"Mm," he said. "Well, if that means having the Kruegers out for dinner, or anything like that, you'd better forget about it right now. I don't want that phony little son of a bitch in my house."

And so there was no one in the house but themselves. They were isolated. Jack had set up his work table in a corner of the main room and he sat there for most of the day, hunched over his pencil.

"You ought to use the *little* room for working," she said. "Wouldn't that be better?"

"No. I like being able to look up and see you. Moving in and out of the kitchen, hauling the vacuum cleaner, whatever the hell you're doing. Lets me know you're really here."

One morning, when the housework was done, she brought out her portable typewriter and set it up as far as possible across the room from him.

A NEW YORKER DISCOVERS THE MIDDLE WEST

Except for parts of New Jersey, and maybe Pennsylvania, I had always pictured everything between the Hudson River and the Rockies as a wasteland.

"Writing a letter?" Jack inquired.

"No; something else. Just a sort of idea I have. Does the typewriter bother you?"

"Course not."

The idea had been simmering in her mind for days, complete with that title and that lead; now she settled down to work.

There was Chicago, of course, a gritty and inadequate oasis to the north, and there were isolated spots like Madison, Wisconsin, renowned for their quaintly charming imitations of Eastern culture, but for the most part there was nothing to be found "out there" but vast reaches of corn and wheat and stifling ignorance. The cities bustled with people like George F. Babbitt; the numberless small towns were haunted by what F. Scott Fitzgerald called "their interminable inquisitions that spared only the children and the very old."

Was it any wonder that all the famous writers born in the Middle West had fled it as soon as they could? Oh, they might indulge themselves in sad rhapsodies about it afterwards, but that was only nostalgia; you never heard of them going back there to live.

As an Easterner, born in New York itself, I greatly enjoyed showing stray, bewildered Middle Western visitors through my part of the world. Here, I would explain; this is the way we

"Is this idea of yours a big secret?" Jack called from across the room, "Or can you tell me about it?"

"Oh, it's just—I don't know exactly what it is. It might turn into a magazine piece or something."

"Oh?"

"I don't know. I'm just fooling around."

"Good," he said. "That's what I'm doing, too."

On Mondays and Thursdays he disappeared into the campus, and when he came back he was always on edge—either chagrined or exhilarated, depending on how his class had gone.

"Ah, these kids," he grumbled once, pouring himself a drink, "these fucking kids. Give 'em half a chance and they'll eat you alive."

He drank too much on the good days, too, but he was better company: "Hell, this job's a breeze, baby, if you don't try too hard. Walk in there and talk about what you know, and they lap it up as if they'd never heard it before."

"Maybe they never *have* heard it before," she said. "I imagine you must be a very good teacher. You've certainly taught me a lot."

"Yeah?" He looked shy and greatly pleased. "About poetry, you mean?"

"About everything. About the world. About life."

And that night they could scarcely wait to be finished with their cooling dinner before they fell into bed.

"Oh, Emily," he said, stroking and fondling her. "Oh, baby, you know what you are? I keep saying 'You're great' and 'You're perfect' and 'You're tremendous,' but none of those words are right. You know what you are? You're magic. You're magic."

He told her she was magic so many times, on so many nights, that she finally said "Jack, I wish you'd stop saying that."

"Why?"

"Just because. It's getting a little old."

" 'Old,' huh? Okay." And he seemed hurt.

But she had never seen him happier than when he came home three hours late on one of his class days, a week or so later. "Sorry, sweetheart," he said. "I got to drinking with some of the kids after school. Did you eat?"

"Not yet; it's all in the oven."

"Damn. I would've called you, but I wasn't watching the time."

"That's all right."

As they ate dried-out pork chops, which he washed down with bourbon and water, he couldn't stop talking. "The damnedest thing: there's this kid Jim Maxwell—have I told you about him?"

"I don't think so."

"Big, burly guy; comes from some godforsaken place in south Texas, wears cowboy boots and all that. He always scares me in class because he's so tough—*and* so smart. Damn good poet, too, at least he will be soon. Anyway, to-night he waited until all the other kids'd left the bar, so it was just the two of us having one last round, and he gave me this very squinty look and said he had something to tell me. Then he said—damn, baby, this is too much—he said that when he read my first book it changed his life. Isn't that the God damnedest thing?"

"Well," she said. "That's a great compliment."

"No, but I mean I can't get over it. Can you imagine me

writing anything that could change the life of some total stranger in south *Texas*?" And he forked a slice of pork chop into his mouth and chewed it mightily, savoring his pleasure.

By November he had come to admit, or rather to insist, that his own work wasn't going well at all. He would get up from his desk many times a day to stalk the floor, flipping cigarette butts into the fireplace (the bed of ashes in the fireplace became so choked with cigarette butts that only a roaring log fire would burn them out), and saying things like "Who the hell ever said I was supposed to be a poet anyway?"

"Can I read some of what you've been working on?" she asked once.

"No. You'd only lose what little respect for me you have left. You know what it's like? It's like bad light verse. Not even *good* light verse. Dum de dum de dum, and dum de diddly poo. I should've been a songwriter in the nineteen thirties, only I probably would've failed even at that. It'd take about twenty-seven of me to make an Irving Berlin." He stood slumped and staring out the big window at the yellowed grass and naked trees. "I read an interview with Irving Berlin once," he said. "The guy asked him what his greatest fear was, and he said 'Some day I'm going to reach for it, and it isn't going to be there.' Well, that's me, baby. I know I had it—I could feel it, the way you feel blood in your veins—and now I reach for it and reach for it, and it isn't there."

Then the long white Middle Western winter settled in. Jack went back to New York to visit his children over Christmas, and she had the little house to herself. It was lonely at first, until she found she rather enjoyed being alone. She tried working on her magazine article, but its dense, clotted paragraphs seemed to be getting nowhere; then on the third day she received an ebullient Christmas letter from her sister. She had been exclusively concerned with Jack Flanders for so long that it was oddly refreshing to sit down with this letter and remember who she was.

> ... All is well at Great Hedges, and all send their love. Tony has been putting in much overtime, so we rarely get to see him. The boys are thriving ...

Sarah's handwriting was still the neat, girlish script she had taught herself in junior high school. ("Well, it's sweet handwriting, dear," Pookie had told her, "but it's a little affected. Never mind, though; it'll develop more sophistication as you get older.") Emily skimmed through the inconsequential parts of the letter until she came to the meat of it:

> As you may know, Pookie has lost her job—the real estate agency went bankrupt—and naturally we've been very concerned about her. But Geoffrey has come up with a very generous solution. He is fixing up the apartment over the garage into a nice little home for her, where she can live rent-free. She is eligible for Social Security. Tony feels it may be a little awkward having her here, and I agree— not that I don't love her, but you know what I mean—but I'm sure we'll all manage.
>
> Now for the other big news: we are about to inherit the Main House! Geoffrey and Edna will be moving back to New York in the spring—she hasn't been at all well, & he is tired of the long commute & wants to be closer to his office. When they move out, we'll move in, and rent out the cottage for some badly needed income. Can you picture me taking care of that enormous place?
>
> I have shelved *George Fall* because it turned out that I

couldn't proceed very far without doing research in Montana. Can you imagine me ever getting to Montana? I am still writing, though, planning a series of humorous sketches about family life—the kind of thing Cornelia Otis Skinner does so well. I admire her work tremendously.

There was more—Sarah always ended her letters on a cheerful note, even if she had to force it—but the essential sadness of the message from St. Charles was clear.

When Jack got home he was filled with high purpose. No more fooling around, he announced. No more drinking too much every night. Above all, no more letting the students' work take up so much of his time. Did she realize he'd let things slide to the point where he was working on student manuscripts almost every day? What kind of nonsense was that?

". . . Because here's the thing, Emily: I did a lot of thinking on this trip. Did me good to get away and kind of put things in perspective. The point is I think I do have a book. And the only thing that stands in the way of getting it done by summer—the *only* thing—is my own half-assedness. If I'm careful, and lucky—you have to be lucky as well as careful—I can bring it off."

"Well," she said. "That's wonderful, Jack."

The winter seemed to go on forever. The furnace broke down twice—they had to huddle at the fireplace all day wearing sweaters and coats, with blankets around their shoulders—and the car broke down three times. Even when both were in working order there was a pattern of bleak discomfort to the days. Going into town meant putting on heavy socks and boots, wrapping a muffler up to your chin and shivering until the car heater blew warm, gasoline-scented air in your face, then driving the four treacherous miles on ice and snow, under a sky as close and white as the snow itself.

One day when Emily was finished at the supermarket—she had learned how not to be stultified by the supermarket, how to deal with it in quick, competent movements that brought results—she sat for a long time in the steaming brilliance of the laundromat. She watched the whirl of suds and soaked cloth in the porthole of her machine; then she watched the other customers, trying to guess which were students and which were faculty and which were people from the town. She bought a chocolate bar and it tasted surprisingly good—as if, without her knowing it, sitting here and eating this chocolate was the one thing she had wanted to do all day. Waiting for the drying cycle to end she began to feel a vague dread, but it wasn't until she was at the warm, lint-speckled folding table that she figured it out: she didn't want to go home. And it wasn't the drive through snow and ice she dreaded, it was going home to Jack.

"Ah, that fucking Krueger," he said on slamming into the house one evening in February. "I'd like to kick his balls in, if he has any."

"Bill Krueger, you mean?"

"Yeah, yeah, 'Bill.' The cutesy-poo little bastard with the dimpled chin and the charming wife and the three cutesy-poo little girls." And that was all he said until he'd made himself a drink and finished half of it. Then, with one thumb at his temple and his hand spanning his brow, as if he were afraid to let her see his eyes, he said "Here's the thing, baby. Try to understand. I'm what the kids here call 'traditional.' I like Keats and Yeats and Hopkins and—shit, you know what I like. And Krueger's what they call 'experimental'—he's thrown everything overboard. His favorite critical adjective is 'audacious.' Some kid'll get stoned on pot and scribble out the first thing that comes into his head, and Krueger'll say 'Mm, that's a very audacious line.' His students are all alike, the snottiest, most irresponsible kids in town. They think the way to be a poet is to wear funny clothes and write sideways on the page. Krueger's published three books, got another one coming out this year, and he's in all the fucking magazines all the fucking time. You can't even pick *up* a magazine without finding William Fucking Krueger, and baby here's the kicker—here's the punch line: the little cocksucker is nine years younger than me."

"Oh. Well, so anyway, what happened?"

"Shit. This afternoon was what they call Valentine's Day. That means they pass out 'preference sheets' and the kids all write down which teacher they want for next semester; then the teachers get together afterwards and sort them out. You're not supposed to care about it, of course, and everybody acts very nonchalant, but my God you ought to see the red faces and the trembling hands. Anyway, I lost four of my kids to Krueger. Four. And one of them was Harvey Klein."

"Oh." She didn't know who Harvey Klein was—there were evenings when she didn't listen very carefully—but this was plainly an occasion for solace. "Well, Jack, I can certainly see how that would make you feel bad, but the point is it shouldn't. If I were a student in a place like this, *I'd* want to work with as many different teachers as I could. Doesn't that sound logical?"

"Not very."

"And besides, you didn't come out here to waste your energy hating Krueger—or even teaching Harvey Klein. You came here to get your own work done."

He took his hand away from his forehead, squeezed it into a fist and socked the table, which made her jump. "Right," he said. "Emily, you are absolutely right about that. The damn book is *all* that ought to concern me, every day. Even at this very minute, if I have half an hour before dinner I ought to be over there at the desk working, instead of bleeding on you with a lot of trivial, invidious shit like this. You're right, baby; you're right. I want to thank you for bringing it to my attention."

But he spent the rest of the evening in a silent, impenetrable gloom. It was either that night or a very few nights later that she woke up at three to find him gone from the bed. Then she heard him moving around in the kitchen, dropping ice cubes into a glass. The air around the bed was heavy with smoke, as if he'd lain here smoking for hours.

"Jack?" she called.

"Yeah. Sorry I woke you up."

"That's all right. Come on back to bed."

And he did, but he didn't get in. He sat slumped in his bathrobe in the darkness, drinking, and for a long time the only sound in the house was his occasional hacking cough.

"Oh, this isn't me, baby," he said at last. "This isn't me."

"What do you mean, it isn't you? It seems pretty much like you to me."

"I mean I wish to God you could've known me when I was working on my first book, or even my second. *That* was me. I was stronger then. I knew what the hell I was doing and I did it, and everything else fell into place around that. I didn't snivel and snarl and shout and retch and puke all the time. I didn't walk around like a man without skin, without flesh, worrying about what people *thought* of me. I wasn't—" He lowered his voice to show that this next point would be the most telling and damning of all—"I wasn't forty-three years old."

The coming of spring made everything a little better. For many days there was a warm, deep blue sky; the snow shriveled on the fields and even in the woods, and one morning on his way to school Jack came bursting back into the house to announce that he'd found a crocus in the yard.

They began taking long walks every afternoon, down the dirt road, out across the meadows and under the big trees. They didn't talk much—Jack usually walked with his head down and his hands in his pockets, brooding—but their time outdoors soon became the high point of Emily's day. She looked forward to it as eagerly as Jack looked forward to the drinks they had when they got home. Each afternoon she waited with growing impatience for the hour when she could put on her suede jacket, go over to his desk and say "Want to take a walk?"

"A walk," he would say, throwing down his pencil as if delighted to be rid of it. "By God, that's a great idea."

And the walks were even better after they inherited a dog from some neighbors down the road, a tan-and-white mongrel terrier named Cindy. She would lope along beside them or prance in circles around them, showing off, or go racing into the fields to burrow.

"Look, Jack," Emily said once, clutching his arm. "She's going into that pipe under the road—she wants to go through the whole thing and come out the other *side*." And when the dog emerged muddy and trembling from the far end of the pipe she called "Wonderful, Cindy! Oh, good dog! Good dog!" She clapped her hands. "Wasn't that neat, Jack?"

"Yeah. Sure was."

Their most memorable walk was on a breezy afternoon in April. They had gone farther than usual that day, and heading home across a great rutted field, tired but invigorated, they came to a solitary oak tree that seemed to reach into the sky like an enormous wrist and hand. It compelled them to silence as they stood in its shadow looking up through its branches, and they would both remember that Emily got the idea first. She took off her suede jacket and dropped it on the ground. Then she smiled at him—she thought he looked quite handsome with the wind blowing his hair flat against his forehead—and began unfastening the buttons of her blouse.

In no time at all they were naked and embracing on their knees; then he helped her to lie back on the moist earth, saying "Oh, baby; oh, baby..." And they both knew that Cindy would almost certainly begin to bark if anyone dared to approach this sacred place.

Half an hour later, back in the house, he looked up bashfully from his whiskey and said "Wow. Oh, wow. That was really—that was really something."

"Well," she said, lowering her eyes, and she could feel herself blushing, "what's the point of living in the country if you can't do things like that occasionally?"

It rained almost steadily for the next month. Dead earthworms littered the muddy walk from the door to the car, and last year's leaves were blown flat against the picture window to slide down in its streams. Emily took to spending hours at that window, sometimes reading but more often not, staring out into the rain.

"What do you *see* out there, anyway?" Jack asked her.

"Nothing much. Just thinking, I guess."

"What're you thinking about?"

"I don't know. I ought to take the laundry in."

"Ah, come on; the laundry can wait. All I mean is, if something's troubling you I'd like to know about it."

"No, no," she said. "Nothing's troubling me." And she went to get the laundry together.

When she passed his desk again on her way to the door, hauling the heavy denim bag, he looked up and said "Emily?"

"Mm?"

He was forty-three years old, but at that moment his half-smiling face looked as helpless as a child's. "You still like me?" he asked.

"Oh, of course," she told him, and busied herself with her raincoat.

Near the end of the spring semester he said he thought his book was substantially finished. But it wasn't a triumphant announcement, or even a happy one. "The thing is," he explained, "I don't feel ready to send it off yet. The important work is done, I think, but it needs cutting and pruning and fixing. I think it might be smart to hold it back for the summer. Set a deadline for myself in September and have the whole summer to go over it."

"Well," she said. "Good. You'll have three months without classes."

"I know; but I don't want to stay here. It'll get hot as a bitch and it'll be dead. Besides, do you realize how much money we've got in the bank? We could go damn near anywhere."

She had two quick visions—one of heavy surf crashing on rocks and white sand, East Coast or West, and one of purple, cloud-hung mountain ranges. Would love on a beach or love in the mountains be better than this? "Well," she said, "where do you want to go?"

"That's what I've been leading up to, baby." And the

way he looked now reminded her of her father long ago on Christmas morning, when she and Sarah would tear into the wrappings of gifts that turned out to be exactly what they wanted. "How'd you like to go to Europe?"

They flew well ahead of the earth's turning; Heathrow Airport caught them dazed and trembling and gritty-eyed from lack of sleep at seven o'clock in the morning. There wasn't much to see on the ride into London—it seemed not very different than riding into New York from St. Charles—and the cheap hotel recommended by the travel agency was filled with wary, disoriented tourists like themselves.

Jack Flanders had lived in London with his wife soon after the war, and now he kept remarking on how much everything had changed. "The whole town's so American-looking," he said. "I guess we'll find that pretty much all over." But he insisted that the Underground was great—"Wait'll you see how much better it is than the subways in New York"—and took her out to what he called his old neighborhood, where South Kensington and Chelsea are divided by the Fulham Road.

The bartender at his old pub failed to recognize him, until after Jack had spoken his name and shaken his hand; then he became very hearty, but it was clear from the way he didn't quite meet Jack's eyes that he was pretending.

"The point is I'm too *old* to care whether some half-assed bartender remembers me," Jack said as they drank warm beer at a corner table, well away from the dart game. "And besides, I've always hated Americans who come back from England with corny stories about marvelous little pubs. Let's get out of here."

He took her up a side street to the darkened house whose

basement flat he had once occupied, and he drew away from her to stare at it, slumped and brooding, for a very long time. Emily stood near the curb looking idly up and down the street, which was so quiet she could hear the whir and click of the mechanism for changing the traffic light on the corner. She knew it was silly to be impatient—he might be working on an idea for a poem—but that didn't help increase her patience.

"Son of a bitch," he said quietly on turning away from the building at last. "Memories, memories. This was a mistake, baby, coming to this house; it's really shot me down. Let's get a drink. A real drink, I mean."

But the pubs were closed. "It's okay," he assured her. "There's a little club around this next corner called the Apron Strings; I used to be a member; I think they'll let us in. Might even run into some people I used to know." Instead they ran into a stone-faced West Indian doorman who denied them admission; the club had changed management since Jack's time.

They got into a taxicab and Jack leaned earnestly forward to address the driver. "Can you take us someplace where we can get a drink? I don't mean some clip joint; I mean a decent place where we can get a drink." And when he'd settled back beside Emily for the ride he said "I know you think this is dumb, baby, but if I don't get some whiskey in me tonight I'll *never* get to sleep."

They were greeted in an anteroom by a man in a tuxedo who looked Egyptian or Lebanese. "Is very expensive here," he told them with a kindly, confidential smile. "I would not recommend it." But Jack's thirst won out, and they sat in a dim carpeted cellar where an effeminate young Negro played sloppy cocktail piano, and where the bill for two drinks came to twenty-two dollars.

"Probably one of the all-time dumbest things I've ever done in my life," Jack said as they rode back to the hotel, and when they walked into the lobby they found the bar very much open for business. "Oh, *Jesus*," he said, smiting his temple with the heel of his hand, "that's right—I'd forgotten. Hotel bars stay open late too. Isn't this the God damnedest thing? Well; guess we might as well have a nightcap."

Sipping whiskey she didn't want, hearing the strident dissonance of British and American voices—one handsome young Englishman at the bar reminded her of the way Tony Wilson had looked in 1941—Emily knew she was going to cry. She tried to avert it with a childhood trick that had sometimes worked before—pressing both thumbnails hard into the tender flesh beneath the nails of her index fingers, so that the self-inflicted pain might be greater than the ache of her swelling throat—but it was no use.

"You okay, baby?" Jack inquired. "You look— Oh, Jesus, you look like you're just about to— Wait. Wait'll I pay the check, and we'll— Can you hold it till we get upstairs?"

In their room she cried and cried, while he put his arms around her and stroked her and kissed her shuddering head, saying "Oh, baby, come on, now. I know it was awful, but it was all my fault; besides, it's only twenty-two dollars."

"It isn't the twenty-two dollars," she said.

"Well, the whole lousy evening, then. The way I dragged you out to see that house and went into one of my big self-indulgent depressions; the way I—"

"It isn't you; why do you always think everything's you? It's just—it's just that this is my first night in a foreign country and it's made me feel so—vulnerable." And that was true enough, she decided as she got up from the bed to blow her nose and wash her face, but it was only part of the truth. The rest of it was that she didn't want to travel with a man she didn't love.

Paris was better: everything looked just like the photographs of Paris she had studied all her life, and she wanted to walk for hours. "Aren't you getting tired?" Jack would say, lagging behind. He had lived here too, in the old days, but now as he trudged along with a look of petulant bewilderment in his eyes he was the picture of a bumbling American tourist. When they walked into the vast silence of Notre Dame she had to thrust two fingers in the back of his belt to restrain him from walking right into the little cluster of chairs where people were praying.

They had planned on an extended stay in Cannes, so that Jack could work. He said he'd done some of the best work of his life in Cannes; it held a sentimental attraction for him. Besides, it would be practical: she could be out at the beach all day while he secluded himself.

And she did enjoy the beach. She loved to swim, and she was willing to admit she liked the stares of approval she received from suntanned Frenchmen at the way she looked in her bikini. Thin, yes, they seemed to say; small-breasted, certainly; but nice. Very nice.

When her day was over she would go back to the hotel and find their room blue and acrid with cigarette smoke. "How'd it go?" she would ask.

"Terrible." He'd be up and pacing, looking haggard. "You know something? A book of poems is no stronger than its weakest poem. And some of these—five or six of them—are so weak they're going to drag the others down. The whole damn book's going to sink like a stone."

"Take a day off. Come to the beach tomorrow."

"No, no; that won't help."

Nothing would help, and for days he fussed and grumbled. At last he said "It's too expensive here anyway; we're spending a fortune. We could try Italy, or Spain."

And they tried both.

She liked the architecture and sculpture of Florence—she kept seeing things she'd learned about in art-history classes long ago—and in the shops and stalls around the covered bridge she bought small gifts for Pookie and Sarah and the boys; but Rome was hot enough to melt your eyeballs. She almost fainted on her way to visit the Sistine Chapel: she had to sway and stagger into an unfriendly cafe for a glass of water; she had to sit staring into a Coca-Cola for a long time before she gathered strength to go back to the stifling hotel, where Jack was waiting with a pencil behind his ear and another one clamped in his teeth.

They both insisted they liked Barcelona—it had trees and sea breezes; they found a cool room within their price range, and there were good places to sit and have a beer in the afternoons—but Madrid was as inscrutable and unyielding as London. The only good thing about Madrid, Jack said, was the bar at their hotel, where you always got a generous shot-and-a-half in your glass when you ordered "whiskey escoso."

Then they were in Lisbon, and it was time to go home.

Nothing had changed in Iowa City. The sight of their little house, and then of the big room inside it, called up vivid memories of the year before: it was as if they had never been away.

Emily drove off to pick up Cindy from the house where they'd boarded her, and when the dog recognized her, wagging and quivering and showing her teeth, she realized she'd been looking forward to this moment all summer.

In October Jack said "Remember I said I'd set a September deadline for myself? That ought to teach you to trust me and my half-assed deadlines."

"Why don't you send it off the way it is?" she said. "A good editor could help you weed out the weak poems; maybe he could even help you make them better."

"Nah, nah, no editor's that good. Anyway it isn't just a few poems that're weak; the whole book has a sickly, neurotic cast to it. If I had the guts to let you read it you'd see what I mean. I'm going to do *one* thing you suggested, though. I'm going to move my stuff into the little room, and work there."

That was an improvement: she no longer had to feel he was watching her all day.

Soon after he started working in the little room she went in there to clean up, while he was gone at school, and tried to shift the placement of a heavy cardboard box containing winter clothes. It tipped and came open, and she found a fifth of bourbon, half full, that had lain hidden in the folds of an overcoat. She considered taking it out and putting it among the official bottles in the kitchen cabinet, but in the end she laid it carefully back where it seemed to belong.

She resurrected the manuscript of *A New Yorker Discovers the Middle West* and worked fairly steadily on it for some days, but she couldn't make it cohere. The trouble, she decided, was that the essential point of the article was a lie: she *hadn't* discovered the Middle West, any more than she had discovered Europe.

One Sunday morning she sat in the rocking chair in her robe, with Cindy sprawled across her lap. She held her breakfast coffee mug in one hand, stroking Cindy's bristly fur with the other, and she sang a childhood song in a small voice, scarcely aware of singing at all:

> How do you do, my Cindy?
> How do you do today?
> Won't you be my partner?
> I will show you the way.

"Know what?" Jack said, smiling at her from the breakfast table. "The way you carry on with that dog, anybody'd say you want a baby."

She was startled. "A baby?"

"Sure." He got up and came to stand beside her, and his fingers began to play with a lock of her hair. "Doesn't every woman want a baby sometime?"

The advantage of being seated, while he stood over her, was that she didn't have to meet his eyes. "Oh, I don't know," she said. "Sure, I guess so; sometime."

"It might be pointed out," he said, "that you're not getting any younger."

"What's all this *about*, Jack?"

"Let Cindy get down. Stand up. Come and give me a hug. Then I'll tell you." He wrapped her close in his arms and she put her head against his chest, so that it still was not required to look at his eyes. "Listen," he said. "When I got married I didn't know what I was doing; did it for all the wrong reasons; and for years now, ever since the divorce, I've been saying I'd never do it again. But the point is you've changed all that, Emily. Listen. Not now—oh, not now, baby, but soon—as soon as the damn book's done—do you think you might consider marrying me?"

He took both her hands and held her at arms' length.

His eyes were shining, and his mouth was curling into a shape of shyness and pride like that of a boy who's just stolen his first kiss. There was a tiny trickle of egg yolk on his chin.

"Well, I don't know, Jack," she said. "It's a thing I'd have to think about, I guess."

"Okay." He looked hurt. "Okay; I know I'm no prize package."

"It isn't you; it's me. I just don't know if I'm ready for—"

"*Okay*, I said." And after a while he went into the little room and shut the door.

They still took walks nearly every afternoon—the country was rich with autumn foliage—but now it was Emily who tended to walk with her head down, keeping her own counsel, looking at her shoes. Without saying anything about it, they avoided the route that led past the solitary oak tree.

In November she made up her mind to leave him. She would go back to New York but not to *Food Field Observer*; she would find a better job, and a better apartment too; she would embark on a new and better life, and she would be free.

All that remained was breaking the news. She formed the opening phrases in her mind and rehearsed them several times: "Things aren't right, Jack. I think we both know that. I've decided the best thing to do, for both of us, is to . . ." And she sat waiting for him outside the closed door of the little room.

When he came out he moved as if he'd been shot in the back. He sank into the sofa across from her, and she looked at him closely for signs that he might have been nipping from the secret bottle, but he was sober. His eyes were as round as an actor's in the final moments of a tragedy.

"I can't," he announced, barely above a whisper, and she was reminded of the way Andrew Crawford had said "I can't" in bed, years ago.

"Can't what?"

"Can't write."

She had comforted him so often at times like this that now she was empty of all consolation and reassurance; she could only tell him what was true. "I wish you wouldn't say that," she said.

"You do? Well, so do I. I wish a lot of things."

It was clear that she couldn't tell him now. She waited two or three days, until she was damned if she'd wait any longer, and then she said it. "Things aren't right; I think we both know that. I've decided the best thing to do . . ."

She could never afterwards remember how she finished that sentence, or what reply he made to it, or what she said next. She remembered only his brief show of raffish indifference and then his rage, when he shouted and threw a whiskey glass against the wall—he seemed to feel he might get her to stay if only they had a loud enough quarrel—and then his collapse into pleading: "Oh, baby, don't do this; please don't do this to me . . ."

It was two in the morning before she could make a bed for herself on the sofa.

With the fall chilling rapidly into winter, she went back to New York alone.

CHAPTER 3

She knew she was awake because she could see morning light in the pale floating shape of a closed Venetian blind, far away. It wasn't a dream: she was lying naked in bed with a strange man, in a strange place, with no memory of the night before. The man, whoever he was, had a heavy arm and leg flung around her, clamping her down, and in her struggle to free herself she knocked over a bedside table that fell with a crash of broken glass. It didn't wake him, but he groaned and turned away from her; that made it easy to crawl down to the foot of the bed and get out, avoiding the glass, and feel her way along the wall for a light switch. She didn't panic: nothing like this had ever happened to her before, but that didn't mean it would ever happen again. If she could find her clothes and get out of here and get a cab and go home it might still be possible to put the world in order.

When she found the switch the apartment sprang into existence around her, but she didn't recognize it. She still didn't recognize the man, either. He was facing away from her but she could see his profile; she studied it as carefully as if she were making a drawing from life, but it meant nothing. The only familiar things in the room were her clothes, draped over the back of a corduroy armchair not far from where the man's shoes and pants and shirt and underwear lay strewn on the floor. The word "sordid" came into her mind; this was sordid.

She got dressed quickly and found the bathroom, and while combing her hair at the mirror she realized that getting out of here wasn't absolutely essential; there was another alternative. She could take a hot shower and go to the kitchen and make coffee and wait for him to wake up; she could greet him with a pleasant morning smile—a slightly reserved, sophisticated smile—and as they talked she'd be sure to remember everything she had to know: who he was, how they'd met, where she'd been last night. It would all come back, and she might easily decide she liked him. He might make Bloody Marys to ease their hangovers, and take her out for breakfast, and it might turn out to be—

But this was the counsel of irresponsibility, of promiscuity, of sordidness, and she quickly decided against it. Back in the room where he slept she righted the spindly table that had fallen with its load of bottles and glasses. She found a sheet of paper and wrote a note for him, which she propped on the table:

Be careful:
Broken glass on floor.
E.

Then she let herself out of the apartment and was free. It wasn't until she was on the street—it turned out to be Morton Street, near Seventh Avenue—that she felt the weight of all the unaccustomed drinking she must have done last night. The sun assaulted her, sending yellow streaks of pain deep into her skull; she could barely see, and her hand shook badly in trying to open the door of a taxicab. But riding home, inhaling the hot wind that came in through the cab window, she began to feel better. It was Saturday—how could she be so sure it was Saturday when she'd forgotten everything else?—and that gave her two full days of recuperation before she had to go back to work.

It was the summer of 1961, and she was thirty-six.

Soon after coming back from Iowa she'd been hired as a copywriter for a small advertising agency, and she'd become something of a protégée to the woman who ran it. It was a good job, though she would rather have been in journalism, and the best part of it was that she could live in a high, spacious apartment near Gramercy Park.

"Morning, Miss Grimes," said Frank, at the desk. There was nothing in his face to suggest that he might have guessed how she'd spent the night, but she couldn't be sure: she walked through the lobby with a bearing of unusual severity, in case he was following her with his eyes.

The wallpaper of the hallway was patterned in a yellow-on-gray design of rearing horses; she had passed it hundreds of times without a glance, but now the first thing she saw on getting off the elevator was that someone had penciled a long, thick penis jutting out from between one of the horses' hind legs, with big testicles slung beneath it. Her first impulse was to find a pencil eraser and rub it out, but she knew that wouldn't work: it would have to be obliterated with new paper.

Alone and safe behind her own locked door, she took pleasure in finding that everything in her home was clean. She spent half an hour soaping and scrubbing herself in the shower, and while there she began to remember the events of the night. She had gone to the apartment of a married couple she scarcely knew, in the East Sixties, and it had turned out to be a bigger, noisier party than she'd expected—that accounted for the nervousness that had made her drink too fast. She closed her eyes under the pelting of hot water and recalled a sea of talking, laughing people out of which several strangers' faces came up close: a jolly bald man who said the whole preposterous idea of Kennedy for President had been a triumph of money and public relations; a thin, dapper fellow in an expensive suit who said "I understand you're in the ad game too"; and the man who was probably the one she'd slept with, whose earnest voice had talked to her for what seemed like hours and whose plain, heavy-browed face was very likely the face she had studied this morning. But she couldn't remember his name. Ned? Ted? It was something like that.

She put on clean, comfortable clothes and drank coffee —she would have loved a beer but was afraid to open one—and was just beginning to enjoy a sense of her life's coming back to solidity when the telephone rang. He had struggled awake; he had groaned through his own morning ablutions and guzzled a beer; he had found the number she'd probably given him and prepared a courtly little greeting for her, a mixture of apology and reawakened desire. Now he would ask her out for breakfast, or lunch, and she would have to decide what to say. She bit her lip and let the phone ring four times before she picked it up.

"Emmy?" It was her sister Sarah's voice, and it sounded like that of a shy, serious child. "Look, it's about Pookie, and I'm afraid it's bad news."

"Is she dead?"

"No; but she's very— Let me start at the beginning, okay? I hadn't seen her for four or five days, which was sort of strange because she's usually—you know—over here quite a lot, so this morning I sent Eric over to the garage apartment to sort of check on her, and he came running back and said 'Mom, you better get over there.' She was lying on the living-room floor without any clothes on, and at first I thought she *was* dead: I couldn't even tell if she was breathing, but I was pretty sure I could feel a very faint pulse. Another thing: she'd gone to the— Can I be basic?"

"You mean she'd emptied her bowels?"

"That's right."

"Well, Sarah, people do that when they're—"

"I know, but there was a pulse. Anyway, as luck would have it our own doctor is on vacation, and the man filling in for him is this kind of rude young guy I'd never seen before; he examined her and said she was alive but in a coma, and he asked me how old she was and I couldn't tell him—*you* know how Pookie's always been about her age—and he looked around and saw all these empty whiskey bottles and he said 'Well, Mrs. Wilson, nobody lives forever.'"

"Is she in the hospital now?"

"Not yet. He said he'd make arrangements but it might take time. He said we could expect the ambulance some time this afternoon."

It still hadn't come by the time Emily eased herself off

the sweltering train at St. Charles, where Sarah met her in the old Plymouth she shared with her sons. "*Oh*, I'm so glad you're here, Emmy," she said. "I feel better about everything already." And driving very slowly, puzzling over the gearshift and the floor pedals as if she'd never quite mastered the knack of them, she began to take her sister home.

"It's funny," Emily said as they passed a giant pink-and-white shopping center. "When I first came out here this was all open country."

"Things change, dear," Sarah said.

But nothing was changed about the old Wilson place, except that tall weeds had long eclipsed the little GREAT HEDGES sign. Tony's maroon Thunderbird stood glistening in the driveway. He bought himself a new one every other year, and nobody else was allowed to drive it; Sarah had explained once that this was his sole extravagance.

"Is Tony home?" Emily asked.

"No; he went off fishing for the day with some of the guys from Magnum. He doesn't even know about any of this yet." Then, after she'd parked at a respectful distance from the Thunderbird and gotten out to stand frowning over the car keys in her hand, she said "Look, Emmy, I know you must be starving but I think we ought to look in on Pookie first. I mean I don't want to have her just *lying* there, okay?"

"Sure," Emily said. "Sure; of course." And they walked on crunching gravel to the sunbaked box of the "garage," whose garage space was too narrow for modern automobiles. Emily had visited her mother in the upstairs apartment several times—listening to her talk for hours under the close beaverboard ceiling, staring at photographs of herself and Sarah as children on the smudged beaverboard walls, waiting for the first possible chance of escape—but nothing prepared her for what she found now at the top of the creaking stairs.

The naked old woman lay face down, as if she'd tripped on the rug and fallen forward. The heat of the place was all but unbearable—she might easily have collapsed from the heat alone—and it was true about the whiskey bottles: there were six or eight of them around the room, all "Bellows Partners' Choice" and all empty. (Had she been embarrassed to put so many bottles into the trash for one of the boys to remove?)

"Girls, I'm terribly sorry about all this," she seemed to be saying. "Isn't there something we can do?"

"Do you think we could get her into bed?" Sarah said. "For when the ambulance comes?"

"Right. Good idea."

First they prepared the bedroom. The tangled sheets looked as if they hadn't been changed for many weeks, and Sarah couldn't find clean ones, but they did their best to make the bed presentable; then they went back to get her. They were both sweating freely by this time and breathing hard. Crouching, they eased her over on her back. Emily took her under the armpits and Sarah under the knees, and they carried her. She was small but very heavy.

"Careful of this door frame," Sarah said, "it's narrow."

They sat her on the bed and held her upright while Sarah worked with a comb at her sparse hair.

"Never mind that, dear," she seemed to say as her loose head wobbled under the comb. "I can do that later. Just cover me. Cover me."

"There," Sarah said. "That's a little better. Now, if you can sort of turn her, I'll bring her feet up and we'll—that's it—easy; easy—there."

She was lying face-up with her head on the pillow, and her daughters stood back from the ugly old body with a sense of relief and accomplishment.

"You know something?" Sarah said brightly. "I'd give a lot to have that good a figure when *I'm* her age."

"Mm. Does she have a nightgown or something?"

"I don't know; let's look."

All they could find was a light summer robe that was almost clean. Stooping and jostling each other, they worked a sleeve of it up one soft arm and stuffed the flimsy cloth under her back to bring the other sleeve into place; when the robe was finally closed and fastened their mother was dressed, and they drew the top sheet up to her chin.

"Well, I can tell you it hasn't been easy," Sarah said as they went back into the living room to gather up the whiskey bottles. "It hasn't been easy having her here over the past—what's it been now, four years?"

"I can imagine."

"I mean *look* at this place." Holding three or four bottles in one arm, she used her free hand to gesture around the apartment. Every surface in sight was filmed with grime. The ashtrays were heaped to overflowing with very short cigarette butts. "And come here; look at this." She led Emily into the bathroom and pointed down the toilet bowl, which was brown both above and below the water-line. "*Oh*, if only she could have stayed in the city," Sarah said, "with things to do and people to see. Because the thing is there was never anything for her to *do* out here. She'd always be over at the house, and she wouldn't watch television; she wouldn't let *us* watch television; she'd talk and talk and talk until Tony was nearly out of his mind, and she'd—she'd—"

"I know, baby," Emily said.

They went downstairs—the fresh air felt good, even in the heat—and carried their armloads of whiskey bottles to the kitchen door of the main house, where they pressed them deep into a garbage can that was crawling with flies.

"You know what I think?" Sarah said as they sat exhausted at the kitchen table. "I think we both deserve a drink."

The ambulance arrived in midafternoon—four quick, vigorous young men in gleaming white who seemed to enjoy their work. They strapped the old woman into an aluminum stretcher, brought her downstairs with swift delicacy, shoved her inside their vehicle and slammed its doors and were gone.

That evening Sarah drove Emily to the hospital, where a tired-looking doctor explained the nature of a cerebral hemorrhage. Their mother might die in the next day or so, he said, or she might live for a good many years with severe brain damage. In the latter case, she would probably have to be institutionalized.

"... And of course institutions cost money," Sarah said as they rode slowly homeward through the clean new suburbs, "and we haven't *got* any money."

EAT, said a big electric sign just ahead; beneath it, in smaller letters, was the word COCKTAILS, and Sarah steered the old Plymouth into the parking lot.

"I didn't feel like going home just yet anyway," she said, "did you?" When they were settled in a slick booth inside she said "I really wanted the air-conditioning more than the drink; doesn't it feel wonderful?" Then she raised her glass for a toast, looking suddenly very young, and said "Here's to Pookie's making a full recovery."

"Well," Emily said, "I don't think we'd better count on anything like that, Sarah. The doctor said—"

"I know what he said," she insisted, "but I know Pookie, too. She's a remarkable woman. She's tough. *I* bet she bounces back from this. Just wait and see."

There was no point in arguing; Emily agreed that they would wait and see. For a little while there was no talk at all, and Emily used the silence to dwell with bewilderment and chagrin on the way she had woken up this morning. Ned? Ted? Would she ever figure it out? Had she had what drunks call a blackout?

When she came into focus on her sister's face again it was bright with proud talk about Peter, who would be starting college in the fall, and who viewed college only as a necessary preparation for being accepted into General Theological Seminary.

". . . All these years, and his ambition hasn't wavered once. That's what he wants to do, and he's going to do it. He's a remarkable boy."

"Mm. And how about Tony Junior? He must've finished high school last year."

"That's right; except the thing is he didn't graduate."

"Oh? You mean his grades weren't good enough?"

"That's right. Oh, he *could* have graduated, but he spent practically the whole year running around with this —haven't I told you about that?"

"A girl, you mean?"

"She's not a girl, that's the whole point. She's thirty-five years *old*. She's divorced and she's rich and she's ruining him. Ruining him. I can't even talk to him any more, and neither can his father. Even Peter can't talk to him."

"Oh, well," Emily said, "a lot of boys go through things like that. I imagine he'll be all right. Probably be a good thing for him, in the long run."

"That's what his father says." Sarah looked pensively into her glass. "And Eric—well, Eric's sort of like Tony Junior. Sort of like his father, too, I suppose. Never been a student; all he cares about is cars."

"Are you—getting any writing done, Sarah?"

"Oh, not really. I've more or less given up on the humorous family-life sketches. I did four of them, but Tony said they weren't funny. He said they were good—well-written, good details, held your interest and all that—but he said they weren't funny. Maybe I was trying too hard."

"Could I read them sometime?"

"Sure, if you want to. Only you probably won't think they're funny either. I don't know. Humor is a lot harder than—you know—serious stuff. Harder for me, anyway."

And Emily's mind went away again, thinking of her own troubles; she returned only when she realized that Sarah had brought the conversation around to money.

". . . And have you any idea what Tony's take-home pay from Magnum is?" she was saying. "Wait, look; here, I'll show you." She rummaged in her purse. "Here's the stub from his last paycheck. Just look."

Emily had expected it wouldn't be much, but even so she was surprised: it was a little less than she earned at the advertising agency.

"And he's worked there twenty-one years," Sarah said. "Can you imagine? It's that old, old, stupid old business of the college degree, you see. All the men his age with engineering degrees are in top management now. Of course Tony has a supervisory position too, but it's much lower down in the—you know—in the organization. Our only other income is the rent from the cottage, and most of that goes into upkeep. And have you any idea of the *taxes* we pay?"

"I guess I've always thought old Geoffrey helped you out to some extent."

"Geoffrey's poorer than we are, dear. That little import office barely pays their rent in the city, and Edna's been very sick."

"So there isn't any—inheritance, or anything."

"Inheritance? Oh, no. There's never been anything like that."

"Well, Sarah, how do you manage?"

"Oh, we do. Just barely, but we manage. On the first of every month I sit down at the dining-room table—and I make the boys sit down with me too, at least I did when they were younger; it's been good for them to learn about handling money—and I divide everything into accounts. First and foremost is the G. H. account. That covers—"

" 'G. H.'?"

"Great Hedges," Sarah said.

"Why do you call the place that?"

"What do you mean? It's *al*ways been called—"

"Pookie gave it that name, baby. I was there when she thought it up."

"She did?" And Sarah looked so stunned that Emily was sorry she'd said it. They both reached for their drinks.

"Look, Sarah," Emily began. "It's probably none of my business, but why don't you and Tony sell that place? The houses wouldn't be worth anything, but think of the land. You've got eight acres in one of the fastest-growing parts of Long Island. You could probably get—"

Sarah was shaking her head. "No; no, that's out of the question. We couldn't do that; it wouldn't be fair to the boys. They love the place, you see. It's their home. It's the only home they've ever known. Remember how awful it was when we were little? Never having a—"

"But the boys are *grown*," Emily said, and the alcohol was beginning to work in her: she spoke more sharply than she'd meant to. "They'll all be leaving soon. Isn't it time for you and Tony to think of yourselves? The point is you could get a good, efficient modern house for *half* what you're spending on—"

"That's another thing," Sarah said. "Even if it weren't for the boys, I can't quite picture Tony and me in some pedantic little—"

" 'Pedantic'?"

"*You* know, some conventional little ranch house like all the others."

"That isn't what 'pedantic' means."

"It isn't? I thought it meant conventional. Anyway, I don't see how we could ever do a thing like that."

"Why not?"

The argument went on for half an hour, going over and over the same ground, until in the end, when they were getting up to go back to the car, Sarah suddenly gave in. "Oh, you're right, Emmy," she said. "It *would* be good for us to sell the place. Good for the boys, too. There's just one hitch."

"What's that?"

"You'd never convince Tony."

Back at the house they walked through the garbage-smelling kitchen, through the dining room, across the musty, creaking living room—where Emily always expected to find old Edna curled up and smiling on the sofa —and into what Sarah called the den, where Tony and Peter were watching television.

"Hi, Aunt Emmy," Peter said in a manly voice, getting to his feet.

Tony rose slowly, as if reluctant to leave the screen, and came forward with a can of beer in his hand. He was still in his fishing clothes, speckled with bait stains, and his face was bright with sunburn. "I say," he said. "I'm ve'y sorry about Pewkeh."

Peter turned off the booming television and Sarah gave them a full report on what the doctor had said, concluding with her own fact-defying prognosis: "*I* bet she bounces back."

"Mm," Tony said.

For hours that night—long after Tony and Peter had gone to bed, long after Eric and even Tony Junior had come slouching in with mumbled greetings for their aunt and mumbled expressions of sorrow about their grandmother—the Grimes sisters stayed up to talk and drink. They started out in the den and later moved into the living room, which Sarah said was cooler. There Emily sat cross-legged on the floor, for easy access to the liquor on the coffee table, and Sarah sank into the sofa.

"... And I'll never forget Tenafly," Sarah was saying. "Remember when we lived in Tenafly? In that sort of stucco house with the bathroom on the ground floor?"

"Sure I remember."

"I was nine then and you must have been about five; it was the first place we lived after the divorce. Anyway, Daddy came out to visit us there once, and after you were in bed he took me out for a walk. We went to the drugstore and had black-and-white ice-cream sodas. And on the way home—I can still remember that street, the way it curved around—on the way home he said 'Baby, can I ask you a question?' Then he said 'Who do you love more, your mother or me?' "

"My God. Did he really say that? And what did you say?"

"I told him—" Sarah sniffled. "I told him I'd have to think it over. Oh, I knew, of course"—her voice wavered out of control, but she recovered it—"I knew I loved him much, much more than Pookie, but it seemed terribly disloyal to Pookie to come right out and say it. So I said I'd think it over and tell him the next day. He said 'You promise? If I call you on the telephone tomorrow, will you tell me then?' And I promised. I remember not being able to look Pookie in the face that night and not sleeping very well, but when he called up I told him. I said 'You, Daddy,' and I thought he was going to cry, right there on the phone. He used to cry a lot, you know."

"He did? I never saw him cry."

"Well, he did. He was a very emotional man. Anyway, he said 'That's wonderful, sweetheart,' and I remember being relieved that he wasn't crying. Then he said 'Listen. As soon as I can arrange a few things I'm going to have you come and live with me. It might not be right away but it'll be soon, and we'll be together always.' "

"God," Emily said. "And then of course he never did anything about it."

"Oh, I stopped expecting it to happen after a while; I stopped thinking about it."

"And you had to go on living with Pookie and me." Emily fumbled for a cigarette. "I had no idea you went through anything like that."

"Oh, don't misunderstand," Sarah said. "He loved you too; he always used to ask me about you, especially later, when you were growing up—what you were like, what you'd like for your birthday—*you* know. It's just that he never really got to know you very well."

"I know." Emily took a drink, finding her keen sense of melancholy enhanced by the way the alcohol seemed to go straight from the roof of her mouth into her veins. She had a story of her own to tell now; it might not be as sad a story as Sarah's, but it would do. "Remember Larchmont?" she began.

"Sure."

"Well, when Daddy came out for Christmas that year . . ." She told of how she'd lain awake to hear her parents talking and talking downstairs and how she'd called out for her mother, who had come up smelling of gin and said they were "coming to a new understanding," and how all hope had been lost the next day.

Sarah was nodding in corroboration. "I know," she said. "I remember that night. I was awake too. I heard you call out."

"You did?"

"And I heard Pookie come up. I was as excited as you were. And then a little later, maybe half an hour later, I got up and went downstairs."

"You went downstairs?"

"And there wasn't much light in the living room, but I could see them lying together on the sofa."

Emily swallowed. "You mean they were—getting laid?"

"Well, there wasn't much light, but he was on top and it was—you know—it was a very passionate embrace." And Sarah brought her glass up quickly to hide her mouth.

"Oh," Emily said. "I see."

They were both silent for a while. Then Emily said "I

wish you'd told me that a long time ago, Sarah. Or no, come to think of it, I guess I'm glad you didn't. Tell me something else. Have you ever understood why they got divorced? Oh, I know *her* version—she felt 'stifled'; she wanted freedom; she always used to compare herself with the woman in *A Doll's House*."

"*A Doll's House*, right. Well, it was partly that; but then a couple of years after the divorce she decided she wanted to come back to him, and he wouldn't have her."

"You sure?"

"Positive."

"Why?"

"Well, think about it, Emmy. If you were a man, would you have taken her back?"

Emily thought about it. "No. But then, why did he ever marry her in the first place?"

"Oh, he loved her; don't worry about that. He told me once she was the most fascinating woman he'd ever met."

"You're kidding."

"Well, maybe he didn't say 'fascinating.' But he said she cast a spell."

Emily studied the drink in her hand. "When did you *have* all these talks with him, anyway?"

"Oh, mostly during the time I had braces. I didn't *have* to go into the city once a week, you see—the dentist only wanted to see me once a month. That once-a-week story was something Daddy and I made up, so we'd have more time together. Pookie never did figure it out."

"Neither did I." And even now, at thirty-six, Emily was jealous. "And who was Irene Hammond?" she asked. "The lady I met at Daddy's funeral?"

"Oh, Irene Hammond was only around in the last few years, toward the end of his life. There were others."

"There were? Did you meet them?"

"Some of them. Two or three of them."

"Were they nice?"

"One of them I didn't like at all; the others were all right."

"Why do you suppose he never married again?"

"I don't know. He said once—this was when I was engaged to Donald Clellon—he said that a man ought to be happy in his work before he got married, and maybe it was partly that. He was never happy in his work, you see. I mean, he'd wanted to be a great reporter, somebody like Richard Harding Davis, or Heywood Broun. I don't think he ever understood why he was only—you know—only a copy-desk man."

And that did it. They had been holding back tears all evening, all night, but that phrase was too much. Sarah started crying first and Emily got up from the floor to take her in her arms and comfort her, until it was clear that she couldn't comfort anyone because she was crying too. With their mother lying in a coma twenty miles away, they clung together drunkenly and wept for the loss of their father.

Pookie didn't die the next day, or the day after that. By the end of the third day it was assumed that her condition was "stabilized," and Emily decided to go home. She wanted to be back in her air-conditioned apartment, where nothing smelled of mildew and everything was clean, and she wanted to get back to work.

"Pity we don't see more of you, Emmy," Tony said as he drove her swiftly to the station in his Thunderbird. When he parked near the platform to wait for the train, she realized she might never have a better chance than this for bringing up the question of selling the place. She tried to do it tactfully, making clear that she knew it was none of her business, implying that it must surely be something he'd thought about before.

"Oh, God, yes," he said as they heard the sound of the approaching train. "I'd love to be rid of it all. Let them take a bulldozer and bury it. If it were up to me I'd—"

"You mean it *isn't* up to you?"

"Oh, no, pet; it's Sarah, you see. She'd never hear of it."

"But Sarah says she *wants* to do it. She told me *you* were the one who didn't."

"Oh?" he said, looking bemused. "That so?"

The train was on them with an overwhelming noise; there was nothing for Emily to do but say goodbye.

When she got off the elevator at her floor—the great cock and balls still protruded from the wallpaper horse— she was almost too tired to stand. The apartment was as cool and welcoming as she'd known it would be, and she sank into a deep chair with her heels sliding straight out on the floor. This was fatigue. Tomorrow she would ride uptown to Baldwin Advertising, she would do her job with all the intelligence and efficiency they had come to expect of her, and she would drink nothing for a week except a beer or a glass of wine after work each day. In no time at all she would be herself again.

But meanwhile it was only eight o'clock in the evening; there was nothing in the place she wanted to read; nothing to watch on television; nothing to do but sit here and go over and over the time in St. Charles in her mind. After a while she was up and pacing the floor with her fist in her mouth. Then her telephone rang.

"Emily?" said a man's voice. "Oh, wow, are you really there? I've been calling you and calling you."

"Who's this?"

"It's Ted; Ted Banks—Friday night, remember? I've been calling you since Saturday morning—three, four times a day, and you were never home. Are you okay?"

Hearing his voice and his last name brought it all back. She could see his plain, heavy-browed face now and remember the shape and the weight and the feel of him; she could remember everything. "I was out of town for a few days," she said. "My mother was very ill."

"Oh? How is she now?"

"She's—better."

"Good. Look, Emily, first of all I want to apologize— I haven't had that much to drink in years and years. I'm not used to it."

"I'm not either."

"So if I made a total fool of myself I'm terribly—"

"That's okay; we were both pretty foolish." She wasn't tired any more, except in a pleasant, well-earned way. She felt good.

"Well, listen: do you think I could see you again?"

"Sure, Ted."

"Oh, great; that's great. Because I really— When? How soon?"

She looked with pleasure around her apartment. Everything was clean; everything was ready. "Well," she said, "almost anytime, Ted. Why not tonight? Give me half an hour to wash up and change, and then—you know—come on over."

CHAPTER 4

The nursing home, a modest Episcopalian retreat at which the Grimes sisters shared the cost of their mother's care, lay roughly halfway between the city and St. Charles. At first Emily went out there once a month; later she cut it down to three or four times a year. Her first visit, in the autumn after Pookie's collapse, was the most memorable.

"Emmy!" the old woman cried, lying half-raised in her hospital bed. "I *knew* you'd come today!"

At first glance she looked startlingly well—her eyes gleamed and her false teeth were bared in a triumphant smile—but then she began to talk. Her wet mouth labored, slurring syllables in a slow parody of the way she'd talked all her life.

"... And isn't it wonderful how everything's worked out so well for us? Just imagine! Sarah's a real princess, and look at *you*. I always knew there was something special about our family."

"Mm," Emily said. "Well, you're looking fine. How do you feel?"

"Oh, I'm a little tired, but I'm just so happy—so happy and so proud of you both. Especially you, Emmy. Lots of girls marry into European royalty—only, you know something funny? I still haven't learned to pronounce his last name!—but how many ever get to be First Lady?"

"Are you—comfortable here?"

"Oh, it's nice enough—of course I knew it'd be nice, built right into the White House—but I'll tell you something, dear." She lowered her voice to an urgent stage whisper. "Some of these nurses don't know how to behave when they're dealing with the President's mother-in-law. Anyway—" She settled back on her pillow. "Anyway, I know you must be terribly busy; I won't keep you. *He* stopped by to see me the other day."

"He did?"

"Oh, just for a few minutes, after his press conference, and he called me Pookie and gave me a little kiss. Such a handsome figure of a man, with that beautiful smile. He has such—such flair. Just imagine! The youngest man ever elected President in American history."

Emily planned her next sentence carefully. "Pookie," she said, "have you been having a lot of dreams?"

The old woman blinked several times. "Dreams, oh, yes. Sometimes—" She looked suddenly frightened. "Sometimes I have bad dreams, terrible dreams about all kinds of terrible things, but I always wake up." Her face relaxed. "And when I wake up everything's wonderful again . . ."

On her way out of the place, passing the open doors of many murmurous rooms filled with beds and wheelchairs, occasionally glimpsing an ancient person's head, she found a nurses' station where two thick-legged young women in white were drinking coffee and reading magazines.

"Excuse me. I'm Mrs. Grimes's daughter—Mrs. Grimes in Two-F."

One of the nurses said "Oh, you must be Mrs. Kennedy"; the other, with a tired little smile to show she was only kidding, said "Can I have your autograph?"

"That's what I wanted to ask about. Is she always this way?"

"Sometimes; not always."

"Does her doctor know about it?"

"Well, you'd have to ask him. Doctor's only here Tuesday and Friday mornings."

"I see," Emily said. "Well, look: is it better to sort of play along with her in something like this, or to try and—"

"Doesn't make much difference, one way or the other," the nurse said. "I wouldn't worry about it, Mrs.—?"

"Grimes; I'm not married."

The delusion didn't last long. Throughout the winter Pookie seemed to know who she was, most of the time, but her talk was much less coherent. She was able to sit in her chair and even to walk around, though once she splattered the floor with urine. By spring she had turned morose and silent, speaking only to complain of her failing eyesight and the nurses' neglect and the shortage of cigarettes. Once, having demanded that a nurse bring her a lipstick and a mirror, she studied her frowning reflection and daubed a full, crimson mouth on the surface of the mirror.

During that year Emily was promoted to "copy supervisor" of Baldwin Advertising. Hannah Baldwin, a trim and vigorous "gal" in her fifties who liked to have it known that hers was one of the only three agencies in New York run by a woman, told her she had a real future in the business. "We love you, Emily," she said more than once, and Emily had to admit it was reciprocated. Oh, not love, exactly—surely not love on either side—more of a mutual respect and satisfaction. She enjoyed her work.

But she enjoyed her leisure a great deal more. Ted Banks lasted only a few months; the trouble was mainly that they both felt an irresistible urge to drink too much when they were together, as if they didn't want to touch each other sober.

Things were on a much more intelligent footing with Michael Hogan. He was a rugged, energetic, surprisingly gentle man; he ran a small public relations firm, but talked so little about his work that she sometimes forgot what he did for a living, and the best thing about him was that he made almost no emotional demands on her. It couldn't even be said that they were close friends: whole weeks might pass without her hearing from him, or caring, and when he did call ("Emily? Feel like having dinner?") it was as if they'd never been apart. They both liked it that way.

"You know something?" she told him once. "There aren't very many people you can enjoy spending Sunday with."

"Mm" he said. He was shaving, standing just inside the open door of his bathroom; she lay propped on pillows in his big double bed, leafing through his copy of *The New York Times Book Review.*

She turned a page and a photograph of Jack Flanders jumped out at her, looking much older and even sadder than when she'd seen him last. There were pictures of three other men in the same full-page review, which ran under the heading "A Spring Poetry Roundup"; she skimmed the columns quickly and found the part about Jack.

In middle age, the once volatile John Flanders has settled into an amiable acceptance of things as they are—
pierced, time and again, by a sharp regret for things lost.
Days and Nights, his fourth book, displays the careful
craftsmanship we have come to expect of him, but too frequently there is too little else to admire. Are acceptance
and regret enough? For daily living, perhaps—not, one
suspects, for the higher demands of art. This reader misses
the old Flanders fire.

Some of the love poems are affecting, particularly "Iowa
Oak Tree," with its strong, erotic final stanza, and "Proposal of Marriage," with its curious opening lines "I watch
you fooling with the dog and wonder / What does this
girl want from me?" Elsewhere, however, one is tempted
to dismiss poem after poem as commonplace or sentimental.

The long final poem should probably have been cut
from the manuscript before it went to the printer. Even its
title is awkward—"Remembering London Revisited"—and
the work itself performs a bewildering exercise in double
flashback: the poet regrets a time when he stood at a
London doorway regretting still another, earlier time. How
much chagrin can a single poem bear without becoming
ludicrous?

One closes this slim volume with something of the
poet's own regret–within–regret malaise, and with all too
little of his hope.

Turning to the brilliant, audacious new work of William
Krueger, we find what can only be called an embarrassment
of poetic riches. . . .

The buzz of Michael Hogan's electric razor had stopped
some time ago; she looked up and found him peering over
her shoulder.

"What's the deal?" he asked her.

"Nothing; just something here about a man I used to
know."

"Yeah? Which one?"

There were four photographs on the page, she could easily have pointed to one of the others—even Krueger—and Michael Hogan would never know, or care, but she felt a stirring of old loyalty. "Him," she said, touching her forefinger to Jack's face.

"Looks like he just lost his last friend," Michael Hogan said.

One Friday morning Sarah called Emily at the office to inquire, happily, if she was free for lunch.

"You mean you're in town?"

"That's right."

"Fine," Emily said. "What's the occasion?"

"Well, Tony had to come in for a business meeting today, that's part of it, but the main thing is we've got tickets to see Roderick Hamilton in *Come Home, Stranger* tonight, and afterwards we're going backstage to *meet* him."

Roderick Hamilton was a famous English actor whose new play had recently opened in New York. "That's wonderful," Emily said.

"He and Tony went to school together in England, you see—have I ever told you that?"

"Yes, I believe you have."

"And at first Tony was too shy to write to him, but I made him do it, and we got back this really nice, really charming letter saying of course he remembered Tony and wanted to see him again, and wanted to meet me. Isn't that exciting?"

"It certainly is."

"So look. We're staying at the Roosevelt, and Tony'll be gone all day. Why don't you come up here for lunch?

They have this really nice place called the Rough Rider Room."

"Well," Emily said. "That sounds appropriate for a couple of old rough riders like you and me."

"What, dear?"

"Never mind. Would one o'clock suit you?"

When she first walked into the restaurant she thought Sarah hadn't arrived yet—all the tables were filled with strangers—but then she saw that a plump little overdressed matron, sitting alone, was smiling at her.

"Come sit down, dear," Sarah said. "You look wonder-ful."

"So do you," Emily said, but it wasn't true. In St. Charles, wearing country clothes, Sarah might still look her age—which Emily quickly calculated was forty-one—but here she looked older. Her eyes were lined and shadowed and she had a double chin. She was slump-shouldered. She had evidently been undecided about which of several pieces of bright costume jewelry to wear with her cheap beige suit, and had solved the problem by wearing them all. In the past year her teeth had developed heavy brown stains.

"Something from the bar, ladies?" the waiter inquired.

"Oh, yes," Sarah said. "I'd like an extra dry martini, straight up, with a lemon twist."

Emily ordered a glass of white wine ("I have to work this afternoon") and they both tried to relax.

"Do you know," Sarah said, "I was just thinking. This is the first time I've been to New York in nine years. It's funny how everything's changed."

"You ought to get in more often."

"I know; I'd love to; it's just that Tony hates it so. He hates the traffic, and he says everything's too expensive."

"Mm."

"Oh!" Sarah said, brightening again. "Did I tell you we heard from Tony Junior?" Some months ago, having concluded his affair with the divorcée (she had found an older man), Tony Junior had gone off to enlist in the Marine Corps. "He's at Camp Pendleton, California, and he sent us a nice long letter," Sarah said. "Of course Tony's still furious with him—he's even threatened to disin*herit* him—"

"Disinherit him from what?"

"—Well, you know, disown him; but I think the experience'll do him a world of good."

"And how are the other boys?"

"Oh, Peter's busy at college, on the dean's list *every* semester, and Eric—well, it's hard to tell with Eric. He's still mad about cars."

Then the talk turned to their mother, whom Emily hadn't visited for some time. The social worker at the nursing home, Sarah said, had called her to report that Pookie was becoming a discipline problem.

"How do you mean, a discipline problem?"

"Well, he said she does things that upset the other patients. One night about four in the morning she went into some old man's room and said 'Why aren't you ready? Have you forgotten this is our wedding day?' And apparently she went on and on like that, until the old man had to call the nurses to come and take her back."

"Oh, my God."

"No, but he was very nice about it—the social worker, I mean. He just said that if that kind of behavior continues we'll have to take her out of there."

"Well, but where would we—I mean where would we *put* her?"

Sarah was lighting a cigarette. "Central Islip, I guess," she said, exhaling smoke.

"What's that?"

"The State Hospital. It's free. Oh, but I understand it's very nice."

"I see," Emily said.

Over her second martini Sarah made a shy announcement. "I suppose I really shouldn't have this," she said. "My doctor told me I drink too much."

"He did?"

"Oh, it wasn't a grim warning or anything; he just told me to cut down. He said my—you know—my liver's enlarged. *I* don't know. Let's not talk about sad things any more. I hardly ever get to see you, Emmy, and I want to hear all about your job and your love life and everything. Besides, I'm going to meet Roderick *Ham*ilton tonight, and I want to be in a good mood. Let's enjoy ourselves."

But a few minutes later she was gazing wistfully around the room. "It's nice here, isn't it," she said. "This is one of the places Daddy used to take me to, just before he'd put me on the train. Sometimes we'd go to the Biltmore, too, or the Commodore, but this is the place I remember best. The waiters knew him here, and they knew me too. They'd always bring me a double scoop of ice cream, while Daddy had his double scotch, and we'd talk and talk . . ."

Afterwards, Emily couldn't remember whether Sarah drank three martinis or four at that lunch in the Rough Rider Room; she remembered only that she herself was fuddled with wine by the time their chicken à la king arrived, and that Sarah ate very little of her portion. She didn't drink her coffee, either.

"Oh, dear, Emmy," she said. "I guess I'm a little drunk. Isn't that ridiculous? I don't know why I—oh, but it's okay.

I can have a little nap upstairs. I'll have plenty of time before Tony gets back; then we'll have dinner and go to the theater and I'll be fine."

She needed help in getting out of her chair. She needed help in walking across the floor, too—Emily held her high and firmly under one soft arm—and in walking down the corridor to the elevators.

"It's okay, Emmy," she kept saying. "It's okay. I can manage." But Emily didn't let go until they were up in the room, where Sarah tottered a few steps forward and collapsed on the double bed. "I'm fine," she said. "I'll just get a little sleep now, and I'll be fine."

"Don't you want to take your clothes off?"

"That's okay. Don't worry about it. I'll be fine."

And Emily went back to the office for a distracted afternoon's work. It wasn't until nearly five o'clock that she began to feel a guilty pleasure: now that she had seen her sister, it might be many months—maybe years—before she would have to see her again.

This would be an evening alone; and sometimes, when she planned things right, she found she didn't mind being alone at all. First she changed into comfortable clothes and got the materials for her light supper started in the kitchenette, then she fixed herself a drink—never more than two—and watched the *CBS Evening News*. Later, after she'd eaten and washed the dishes, she would sit in her deep chair or lie on her sofa with a book, reading, and the hours would pass uncounted until it was time to go to bed.

When the telephone rang at nine o'clock it startled her, and the weak, plaintive sound of Sarah's voice—"Emmy?"—brought her quickly to her feet. "Look," Sarah said. "I hate to ask you this, but do you think you could come up here? To the hotel?"

"What's the matter? Why aren't you at the theater?"

"I—didn't go. I'll explain it when I see you, okay?"

All the way uptown, in a cab that kept getting caught in traffic jams, Emily tried to keep her mind empty; she was still trying to keep her mind empty when she walked down the long carpeted corridor to Sarah's door, which was an inch or two ajar. She thought of pushing it open, but knocked instead.

"Anthony?" Sarah called in a shy, hopeful voice.

"No, baby, it's me."

"Oh. Come on in, Emmy."

Emily went inside the dark room and let the door click shut behind her. "Are you all right?" she said. "Where's the light?"

"Don't turn it on yet. Let's talk a minute first, okay?"

In the dim blue light of the window Emily could see that Sarah was lying on the bed, the way she'd left her this afternoon, except that now the bed was unmade and she appeared to be wearing only her slip.

"I'm awfully sorry about this, Emmy; I probably shouldn't have called you, but the thing is—well, I'll start at the beginning, okay? When Tony got back here I was still—you know—still drunk, I guess, and we had a terrible fight about it and he said he wasn't going to take me to the play, and he—anyway, he went to the play alone."

"He went to the play alone?"

"That's right. Oh, you can't blame him; I *wasn't* in any condition to meet Roderick Hamilton; that part of it's all my fault. But I just—the point is, you and I had such good talks last summer, and I just called you up because I sort of need someone to talk to."

"I see. Well, I'm glad you did call. Can I turn the light on now?"

"I guess you might as well."

Emily felt along the wall for the light switch, and when she found it the room exploded into clarity. There was blood on the tangled sheets and on the pillow; there was blood down the front of Sarah's slip and all over her swollen, wincing face, and in her hair.

Emily sat down in a chair and shaded her eyes with one hand. "I don't believe this," she said. "I don't believe this for a minute. You mean he *beat* you?"

"That's right. Could I have a cigarette, dear?"

"Well, but Sarah, are you badly hurt? Let me look at you."

"No, don't. Don't come any closer, okay? I'll be all right. If I can just get up and wash my face I'll be—I should've done this before you came." She struggled to her feet and went unsteadily into the bathroom, from which came the sound of water running in the sink. "God," she called back. "Can you imagine *this* face being introduced to Roderick Hamilton backstage?"

"Sarah, look," Emily said when they were together in the bedroom again. "You're going to have to tell me a few things. Has this happened before?"

Sarah had managed to get her face almost clean; she was wearing a robe and smoking a cigarette. "Oh, sure," she said. "Happens all the time. I guess it's been happening once or twice a month for about—well, twenty years. It's not usually as bad as this."

"And you've never told anyone."

"I almost told Geoffrey once, years ago. He saw a bruise on my face and asked me about it and I almost told him, but I thought, No, that would only make *more* trouble. I don't know; I guess I probably would've told Daddy about it, if he'd lived. The boys have seen it happen a few times. Tony

Junior told him once if he ever saw him do it again he'd kill him. He said that to his own father."

There were liquor bottles and an ice bucket on a low cabinet against the wall, and Emily looked at them with longing. All she had to do was make herself a drink—and she wanted a strong one—but she willed herself to stay in her chair, still shading her eyes with her hand as if unable to look her sister full in the face. "Oh, Sarah," she said. "Oh, Sarah. Why do you put up with it?"

"It's a marriage," Sarah said. "If you want to stay married, you learn to put up with things. Besides, I love the guy."

"What do you mean, 'I love the guy'? That sounds like a line out of some corny— How can you 'love' someone who treats you like—"

A key scraped and turned in the lock, and Emily stood up to face him. She had her opening words prepared and ready.

He came in blinking in surprise at seeing her. His expressionless face looked a little drunk, and he was dressed for the evening in a dark summer suit that Sarah had probably picked out in some cheap suburban department store.

"How was the play, you son of a bitch?" Emily asked him.

"Don't, Emmy." Sarah said.

"Don't *what*? Isn't it about time somebody talked straight around here? How was Roderick Hamilton, you bullying, wife-beating bastard?"

Tony ignored her, moving past her with the look of a despised little boy ignoring his tormentors, but the room was so small that he had to brush against her on his way to the liquor cabinet. He set out three generous, hotel-room water tumblers and began pouring whiskey.

His silence didn't faze her, and she decided that if he

handed her a drink she would throw it in his face, but first she had a few more things to say. "You're a Neanderthal," she told him, remembering what Andrew Crawford had called him long ago. "You're a pig. And I swear—are you listening to me? I swear to God if you ever touch my sister again I'll—" There was no way to finish that sentence except to repeat Tony Junior's threat, and she repeated it: "I'll kill you."

She drank—apparently he *had* handed her a drink, and apparently she'd accepted it without thinking—and only now, with the alcohol spreading warm through her chest and down her arms, did she begin to realize how much she was enjoying herself. It was fine to be passionately in the right on so clear an issue—the scrappy kid sister as avenging angel; she wanted this exhilaration to go on and on. Glancing over at Sarah, though, she wished Sarah hadn't washed her face and covered her slip and straightened up the bedclothes to hide the bloodstains; it would have made a more dramatic picture the other way.

"It's okay, Emmy," Sarah said in the same calming, understanding way she had always said it in childhood when Emily was out of control. Sarah had a drink in her hand now too; for a moment Emily was afraid she might have to stand here and watch while Tony sat down on the bed beside his wife and they performed the old smiling, arm-entwining ritual from Anatole's, but that didn't happen.

Tony seemed to draw composure from Sarah's "It's okay, Emmy"; he looked into Emily's eyes for the first time, with an infuriating suggestion of a smile, and said "Not really ve'y much one can say, is there? Won't you sit down?"

"I will *not* sit down," she answered, and immediately spoiled the effect of that line by taking another long drink from her glass. The high pleasure of the confrontation was gone. She felt like a strident intruder in something that was none of her business. She managed to get off a few more plangent statements before leaving—things she couldn't remember afterwards, probably repeating her own and Tony Junior's hollow threat of murder—and she asked Sarah several times, with what sounded like fake solicitude, if she was sure she'd be "all right"; then she was out in the elevator and then she was home, feeling like a fool.

It took a great effort of will to keep from calling Michael Hogan ("It's just that I feel I *can't* be alone tonight," she would have said, "and there's a whole *week*end to get through . . ."); instead she had a few more drinks by herself and went to bed.

The phone rang late the next morning and she was almost sure it would be Michael Hogan ("Feel like having dinner?") but it wasn't.

"Emmy?"

"Sarah? Are you all right? Where are you?"

"Downtown—I'm in a phone booth. Tony drove on back, but I told him I wanted to stay in the city. I wanted to sort of think things over. I've been sitting in the park and—"

"Sitting in the park?"

"Washington Square. It's funny how everything's changed. I didn't know our old house was gone."

"That whole block was torn down years ago," Emily said, "when they built the Student Center."

"Oh. Well, I didn't know that. Anyway, if you don't have any special plans I thought maybe you might come down and meet me here. We could have breakfast, or brunch or something."

"Well," Emily said, "sure. Where will I find you?"

"I'll be in the park, okay? On one of the benches right near where the old house used to be. You don't have to hurry; take your time."

On the way downtown Emily weighed the possibilities. If Sarah had left her husband she might want to stay with her sister for a while—maybe a long while—which would inconvenience Michael Hogan. Still, Michael did have an apartment of his own; they could work something out. On the other hand, maybe she *was* only "thinking things over"; maybe she would go back to St. Charles tonight.

The park was filled with baby carriages and with laughing, athletic young men throwing frisbees. Its whole design had changed—the paths ran in different directions now—but Emily had no trouble remembering, in passing, the approximate place where Warren Maddock, or Maddox, had picked her up.

Sarah looked as pathetic on her bench as Emily had expected—small and dowdy in her wrinkled beige, lifting her soft, bruised face to the sun and almost visibly savoring visions of another time.

Emily took her to a cool, decent coffee shop (she knew that if they went to a real restaurant there would be irresistible Bloody Marys, or beers) and for an hour or two they talked in circles.

"... We're not getting anywhere, Sarah," she said at last. "You say you know you ought to leave him; you even say you *want* to leave him, and then when we start going into the practical aspects of that you come back to this business of 'I love the guy.' We're talking in circles."

Sarah looked down at the congealed remains of egg and sausage on her plate. "I know," she said. "I always talk in circles, and you always talk in a straight line. I wish I had your mind."

"It isn't a question of 'mind,' Sarah, it's just—"

"Yes it is. We're a lot different, you and me. I'm not saying one way of looking at things is better than the other, it's just that I've always thought of marriage as being—well, sacred. I don't expect other people to feel that way, but it's the way I am. I was a virgin when I got married and I've been a virgin ever since. I mean," she added quickly, "*you* know—I've never played around or anything." With the words "played around or anything" she brought her cigarette quickly to her lips and squinted over it, either to hide embarrassment or to suggest a veiled sophistication.

"Well, fine," Emily said. "But even if marriage *is* sacred, doesn't that imply that both parties ought to agree on it? What's sacred about the way Tony treats you?"

"He does the best he can, Emmy. I know that may sound funny, but it's true."

Emily exhaled a great cloud of smoke and sat back to look around the coffee shop. In a booth across the aisle a couple of young lovers were murmuring, side by side, the girl's fingers tracing little elliptical patterns on the inner thigh of the boy's tight, well-faded blue jeans.

"Listen, Sarah," she said. "Let's take this whole discussion back to where we were a few minutes ago. You can stay at my place as long as you like. We can work together at finding you a place of your own, and a job. And you don't have to think of it as a permanent separation; think of it as—"

"I know, dear, and it's very sweet of you, but there are so many complications. For one thing, what could I possibly *do*?"

"There's any *number* of things you could do," Emily said, though the only thing she could picture was Sarah working as a receptionist in some doctor's or dentist's office. (Where *did* all those pleasant, inefficient middle-aged ladies come from, and how had they gotten their jobs?) "*That's* not important," she hurried on. "The only important thing now is to make up your mind. Either go back to St. Charles, or start a new life for yourself here."

Sarah was silent, as if pretending to think it over for the sake of appearances; then she said "I'd better go back," as Emily had known she would. "I'll take the train back this afternoon."

"Why?" Emily said. "Because he 'needs' you?"

"We need each other."

So it was settled: Sarah would go back; all of Emily's days and nights would be free for Michael Hogan, and for whatever man might follow him in the long succession. She had to admit she was relieved, but it was a relief that couldn't be shown. "And what you're really afraid of," she said, intending it as a kind of taunt, "what you're really afraid of is that Tony might leave *you*."

Sarah lowered her eyes, displaying the fine little blue-white scar. "That's right," she said.

PART THREE

CHAPTER 1

Whenever Emily thought about her sister over the next few years—and it wasn't often—she reminded herself that she'd done her best. She had spoken her mind to Tony, and she'd offered Sarah sanctuary. Could anyone have done more than that?

Sometimes she found that Sarah made an interesting topic of conversation with men.

"I have a sister whose husband beats her all the time," she would say.

"Yeah? Really beats her?"

"Really beats her. Been beating her for twenty years. And do you know a funny thing? I know this sounds awful, talking about my own sister, but I think she sort of enjoys it."

"Enjoys it?"

"Well, maybe she doesn't enjoy it, exactly, but she takes

it in stride. She believes in marriage, you see. She said to me once 'I was a virgin when I got married and I've been a virgin ever since.' Isn't that the damnedest statement you've ever heard?"

When she talked that way with a man—usually half drunk, usually late at night—she would regret it profoundly afterwards; but it wasn't hard to assuage her guilt by vowing that she wouldn't do it again.

Besides, there wasn't time for anxiety. She was busy. Early in 1965 Baldwin Advertising obtained what Hannah Baldwin called a dream account: National Carbon, whose new synthetic fiber Tynol seemed almost certain to revolutionize the fabric industry. "Think what nylon did!" Hannah exulted. "The sky's the limit on this thing, and we've lucked in on the ground floor."

Emily developed a series of ads introducing the fiber, and Hannah loved them. "I think you've got it licked, honey," she said. "We'll knock their eyes out."

But instead there was a troublesome hitch. "I can't imagine what's wrong," Hannah told Emily. "National Carbon's legal counsel just called me; he wants you to go in and talk to him about the campaign. He wouldn't say anything on the phone, but he sounded very grim. His name's Dunninger."

She found him high in a great steel-and-glass tower, alone in his carpeted office. He was big and sturdy, with a heavy jaw and a voice that made her want to curl up and ride in his pocket like a kitten.

"Let me take your coat, Miss Grimes," he said. "Sit down —no, come around here and sit beside me; then we can go over the material together. In general I think it's fine," he began, and as he talked she looked beyond the layouts and pages of copy to explore the whole ample surface of his desk. Its only ornament was a photograph of a lovely dark-haired girl, probably his daughter; they probably lived in Connecticut, and when he got home every day he would play a few fast sets of tennis with her before they went in to shower and change and join Mrs. Dunninger for cocktails in the library. And what would Mrs. Dunninger be like?

". . . There's just one point," he was saying. "One phrase, and unfortunately it's a phrase that appears over and over in your, uh, copy. You say Tynol has 'the natural elegance of wool.' That could easily be construed as misrepresentation, you see, when we're talking about a synthetic. I'm afraid if we let it go we'll have the F.T.C. on our necks."

"I don't get it," Emily said. "If I say 'You have the patience of a saint,' it certainly doesn't mean you *are* one."

"Ah." He leaned back in his chair, smiling at her. "But if I say 'You have the eyes of a strumpet,' there might conceivably be room for doubt."

They sat laughing and talking for longer than their business required, and she couldn't help noticing that he seemed to be happily taking stock of her legs and her body and her face. She was thirty-nine, but his eyes made her feel much younger.

"Is that your daughter?" she said of the photograph.

He looked embarrassed. "No, it's my wife."

And she couldn't say "I'm sorry" or anything like that without making it worse. "Oh," she said. "She's lovely." Then she mumbled that she'd better be going, and stood up.

"I think you'll find 'natural' is the offending word," he said, walking her to the door. "If you can get around that I don't think there'll be any problem."

She told him she would do her best, and as the elevator dropped her back to reality she revised her fantasies: he didn't live in Connecticut; he lived in an East Side penthouse where that beautiful girl pouted and preened in mirrors all day, waiting for him to come home.

"Miss Grimes?" he said on the telephone a very few days later. "Howard Dunninger. I just wondered if you might have lunch with me."

Almost the first thing he told her, as they sipped wine in what she described to herself as a "wonderful" French restaurant, was that he wasn't really married at all: he and his wife had separated three months ago.

"Well, 'separated' is a euphemism," he said. "The fact is she left me. Not for another man; just because she was tired of me—I imagine she'd been tired of me for some time—and she wanted to see what freedom is like. Oh, it's understandable, I suppose. I'm fifty; she's twenty-eight. When we started living together I was forty-two and she was twenty."

"Isn't it a little romantic to keep her picture on your desk?"

"Pure cowardice," he said. "It's been there so long I thought people in the office might think it looked funny if I put it away."

"Where is she now?"

"California. She wanted to put the greatest possible distance between us, you see."

"Do you have any children?"

"Only from my first marriage; that was a long time ago. Two boys. They're grown now."

Chewing fresh French bread and salad, glancing around at the well-dressed, sophisticated-looking people at other tables, Emily realized it would be easy to make love with Howard Dunninger this very afternoon. Hannah wouldn't care if she didn't show up at the office, and surely the general counsel for National Carbon could set his own schedule. They had both outlived the time of trivial responsibilities.

"What time do you want to get back, Emily?" he asked as the waiter set a gleaming little cognac glass beside her coffee.

"Oh, it doesn't matter; no special time."

"Good." His thin lips curled into a shape of shyness. "I've done so damn much of the talking I've hardly gotten to know you. Tell me about yourself."

"Well, there's not really much to tell."

But there was: her autobiography, edited and heightened here and there for dramatic effect, seemed impossible to conclude. She was still talking when he guided her out across the blazing sidewalk and into a taxicab, and when the cab let them off at his apartment building. She stopped talking finally in the elevator—not because she was finished but only because it seemed important to be quiet here.

It wasn't a penthouse, and it wasn't nearly as grand as she'd imagined. It was blue and brown and white and smelled of leather; it was almost ordinary, and its floor seemed to tilt at dangerous angles as he went about the courtly preliminaries: ". . . Can I get you a drink? Sit down over here . . ." No sooner had he sat close beside her on the sofa than they were all over each other, and the sounds of the city nineteen floors below were overwhelmed by the greater sounds of their breathing; when he helped her into the bedroom it was like a long-awaited, well-deserved passage into light and air.

Howard Dunninger filled her life. He was as appealing as Jack Flanders, with none of Jack's terrible dependency; he seemed to make as few demands on her as Michael Hogan; and when she sought comparisons for the way he made her feel in bed, night after night, she had to go all the way back to Lars Ericson.

After the first few weeks they stopped using his apartment—he said he didn't want to be constantly reminded of his wife—and started using hers. That made it easier for her to get to work on time in the morning, and there was another, subtler advantage: when she was a guest in his place there seemed to be a tentative, temporary quality to the thing; when he came to hers it implied a greater commitment. Or did it? The more she thought about this the more she realized that the argument might easily be reversed: when he was the visitor he could always get up and go away.

In any case, her apartment became their home. He was shy at first about moving his things in, but soon one of her bureau drawers was packed with his laundered shirts, and there were three dark suits and a bright cluster of neckties hanging in the closet. She liked to run her hand down the length of those ties, as if they were a heavy silken rope.

Howard owned a Buick convertible, which he kept in a garage uptown, and in good weather they took drives into the country. Once, having started out for Vermont on a Friday afternoon, they drove all the way up to Quebec City, where they checked into the Château Frontenac as if it were a motel; and Sunday night, on the long trip home, they drank French champagne out of Styrofoam cups.

They went to the theater sometimes, and to small drinking places that she'd only read about before, but most evenings they stayed home, as quiet and gentle with each other as people who'd been peacefully married for years. As she often told him—and she knew it might have been wiser not to tell him at all—she had never enjoyed herself so much with anyone.

The trouble was that he was still in love with his wife.

"There!" he said once, when she hadn't even known he was looking at her. "What you did just then—the way you held your hair back with one hand and bent over the coffee table to pick up that glass—that could have been Linda."

"I don't see how I can possibly remind you of her," she said. "After all, she's a young girl and I'm practically forty."

"I know; and you really don't look anything alike, except that she's small-breasted too and you have the same kind of legs, but just once in a while, some of your mannerisms—it's uncanny."

Another time, when he'd come home in a sour mood and drunk a lot of wine with dinner, he sat nursing a bourbon and water for a long time, silent, until he began to talk in a way that suggested he would never stop.

"...No, but you have to understand about Linda," he said. "It wasn't just that she was my wife; she was all I'd ever wanted in a woman. She was—how can I explain it?"

"You don't have to explain it."

"Yes I do. Have to get it straight in my own mind or I'll *never* get over her. Listen. Let me tell you how I met her. Try to understand this, Emily. I was forty-two years old but I felt older. I'd been married and divorced, I'd had what seemed any number of girls; I guess I felt I'd pretty well exhausted my possibilities. I was out in East Hampton for a couple of weeks and somebody asked me to a party. A lighted swimming pool, Japanese lanterns in the trees, Sinatra records piped out from the house—that kind of thing. A mixed crowd: there were a lot of actors who made television commercials, a couple of children's-book illustrators, a couple of writers, a few business types trying to look arty in their burgundy Bermuda shorts. And son of a bitch,

Emily, I turned around and there was this creature lying on this white chaise longue. I'd never seen skin like that, or eyes like that, or lips like that. She was wearing—"

"Are you really going to tell me what she was *wearing*?"

"—wearing a simple, short black dress, and I took a big drink for courage and went over to her and said 'Hi. Are you somebody's wife?' And she looked up at me—she was too shy or I guess too reserved to smile—and she—"

"Oh, Howard, this is silly," Emily said. "You're just going to get yourself all worked up. You really are a terrible romantic."

"All right, I'll keep it as brief as I can. I don't want to bore you."

"You're not 'boring' me; it's just that you're—"

"All right. The point is, the very next night she was in my bed, and every other night after that; when we got back to town she moved all her stuff into my apartment. She was still in college—she went to Barnard, same as you—and when her classes were over every day she'd hurry down to my place in order to be there when I got home. I can't begin to tell you how sweet that was. I'd go home bracing myself, thinking No, it's too good to be true; she won't be there—and she always was. I look back on that time, that first year and a half, as the God damned happiest time of my life."

He was up and walking the floor now with his drink in his hand, and Emily knew better than to interrupt him.

"Then we got married, and I guess that did take the edge off it a little—for her, I think, more than for me. I was still —well, I hate to keep saying 'happy,' but that's the only word for it. Proud, too; enormously proud. I'd take her places, people would congratulate me, and I remember I'd

say 'I don't believe her; I don't believe any of this yet.' Then
of course after a while I did start to believe her; I started
taking her for granted in ways that nobody should ever take
*any*body for granted. In the early years she used to say I
never bored her, and I took it as a great compliment, but I
don't remember her ever saying that toward the end. I'd
probably begun to bore the hell out of her with my vanity
and my posturings and my—I don't know. My self-pity. And
I think that's when she started getting restless, along about
the time I started boring her. God damn it, Emily, how can
I make you understand how nice she was? It's a thing that
can't be described. Tender, loving, and at the same time she
was tough. I don't mean 'tough' in any pejorative sense,
I mean resilient, courageous; she had a wholly unsentimental way of looking at the world. Intelligent! Jesus, it was
almost frightening sometimes how she'd go straight to the
heart of some elusive, complicated thing with an intuitive
insight. She was funny, too—oh, she didn't sit around getting off paralyzing one-liners, it's just that she had a very
sharp eye for the absurdity behind anything pretentious.
She was a great companion. Why do I keep saying 'was'? It's
not as if she were dead. She was a great companion for me
and now she'll be a great companion for some other man—
or men. I imagine she'll try out quite a few men before she
settles down again."

He sank heavily into an armchair, closing his eyes, and
began massaging the thin bridge of his nose with thumb
and forefinger. "And sometimes now when I think of her in
that particular context," he said in a flat, almost dead voice,
"when I picture her out there with some other man, opening
her—opening her legs for him and—"

"Howard I'm not going to let you do this," Emily said,

standing up for emphasis. "It's maudlin. You're acting like a lovesick little boy, and it's very unbecoming. Besides, it's not very—" She wasn't at all sure if she should finish this sentence, but she did "—not very considerate of me."

That brought his eyes open, but he closed them again. "I thought you and I were friends," he said. "I thought the idea was, you were supposed to be able to talk freely with a friend."

"Hasn't it occurred to you that I might be a little jealous?"

"Mm," he said. "No, as a matter of fact that hadn't occurred to me. I don't get it. How can you be jealous of something that's in the past?"

"Oh, *How*ard. Come on, now. What if I spent whole evenings going over all the wonderful, wonderful qualities of different men I've known?" But that question answered itself: she could tell Howard Dunninger anything about any of her men, or all of them, and he wouldn't care.

In December of that year, National Carbon assigned him to California for two weeks.

"And I suppose you'll see Linda out there, won't you?" she said when he was getting ready to leave.

"I don't see how," he said. "I'll be in Los Angeles; she's 'way up north of San Francisco. It's a big state. Besides, I—"

"Besides you what?"

"Besides I what nothing. I can't seem to get this God damned suitcase shut."

It was a bad two weeks—he called her only twice, toward the end—but she survived it; and he really did come home.

Then in February, late one night when they were about to go to bed, Sarah called.

"Emmy? Are you alone?"

"Well, no, actually, I'm—"

"Oh, you're not. I see. I was hoping you would be." The rhythm and texture of Sarah's voice evoked a sharp sense of that terrible old house in St. Charles—the mildew, the chill, the ancestors staring from the walls, the smell of garbage in the kitchen.

"What's the matter, Sarah?"

"Let's put it this way. To quote John Steinbeck, this is the winter of our discontent."

"I don't think that was original with Steinbeck, baby," Emily said. "Has Tony been—?"

"That's right. And I've made a decision, Emmy. I'm not staying here any more. I want to come and stay with you."

"Well, Sarah, the thing is—I'm afraid that wouldn't be possible." She glanced at Howard, who stood in his bathrobe a few feet away, listening and looking interested. She had told him about her sister. "The thing is, I'm not living alone now."

"Oh. You mean you have a—I see. Well, that does complicate things, but I don't care. I'm leaving anyway. I'll stay in an inexpensive hotel or something. Listen, though: do you think you could help me find a job? *I* can write advertising copy too. *I've* always been able to—you know—turn a phrase."

"There's a little more to it than that," Emily said. "It takes quite a few years to get a job like mine. I really think you'd be better off looking for some other kind of work."

"What kind?"

"Well, maybe working as a receptionist, or something like that." There was a pause. "Look, Sarah, are you absolutely sure you want to do this?" Emily held the phone in both hands and chewed her lip, trying to figure out her motives. Not very long ago she had urged her sister to leave home; now she was urging her to stay.

"Oh, I don't know, Emmy," Sarah said. "I guess I'm not absolutely sure of anything. Everything's so—so mixed up."

"Is Tony there?" Emily asked. "Can I talk to him?" And when Tony came on with a drunken-sounding grunt she felt a fine, swift return of the exhilaration she'd known that night in the hotel room. "Listen, Wilson," she began. "I want you to leave my sister alone, is that clear?" As her voice rose and flattened out she understood why she was doing this: she was showing off for Howard. This would prove she wasn't always tender and loving; she could be tough, resilient, courageous; she had a wholly unsentimental way of looking at the world. ". . . I want you to keep your big—your big fucking hands to yourself," she said, "and if I were a man I'd come out there tonight and make you wish you never *had* any hands. Is that clear? Put Sarah back on."

There were muffled scraping sounds, as if heavy furniture had to be moved before Sarah could come back to the telephone. When she did, it was clear at once that she'd changed her mind.

"I'm sorry to bother you with all this, Emmy," she said. "I probably shouldn't have called in the first place. I'll be all right."

"No, listen," Emily said, feeling greatly relieved. "Call me anytime. Please feel free to call me anytime, and meanwhile I'll keep an eye on the 'Help Wanted' ads in the *Times*, okay? It's just that I don't think you'd be very wise to come right *now*, is all."

"No; I don't either. All right, Emmy. Thanks."

When the phone was back in its cradle, Howard handed

her a drink and said "That's terrible. That must've been very hard on you."

"It's just that there isn't anything I can *do*, Howard," she said. She wanted him to take her in his arms, so she could cry against his shoulder, but he made no move toward her.

"Well," he said, "actually, you could let her have this apartment for a while; we could stay up at my place."

"I know; that did occur to me; but the point is the apartment's only the beginning. You have no *idea* how helpless she is—a funny little middle-aged woman with terrible clothes and bad teeth and without a skill to her name—she can't even *type* except with two fingers."

"Oh, well, I imagine there are things she could do. I might even be able to help her find something at National Carbon."

"And she'd be around our necks," Emily said with more bitterness than she'd intended. "We'd never be free of her for a minute if she were here. I don't *want* her, Howard. I know it may sound awful, but I don't *want* her dragging down my life. If you can't understand that I guess it's just too—too complicated to explain."

"Okay," he said, smiling and frowning at the same time. "Okay. Just take it easy."

Several weeks went by before the next call, at about the same time of night, and this time it was Tony who called. He sounded drunk again, and she could hardly hear him because of other slurred male voices in the background, which she realized after a second were the sound of television turned up too loud.

". . . Your sister's in the hospital," Tony's voice said, trying for as neutral a tone as that of a gruff policeman reporting to the victim's next of kin.

"The hospital? What hospital?"

"Central Islip," the voice said; then it added "where she belongs," and the silence was filled only with the muffled boom and rumble of the television voices.

"Oh my God, Howard," Emily said when she'd hung up the phone. "She's in Central *I*slip."

"What's that?"

"It's where my mother is. The state hospital. The insane asylum."

"Well, Emily, listen," Howard said gently. "Her husband couldn't have just *put* her there. If she's been committed there it can only be because some doctor decided to send her in for treatment. This isn't the Nineteenth Century; nobody says 'insane asylum' any more. It's a modern psychiatric hospital, and it's—"

"You don't *know* what it is, Howard. I do. I've been out there to see my mother. It's twenty or maybe fifty enormous brick buildings; even when you're out there you can't comprehend how big it is because there are so many trees. You walk along those paths thinking This isn't so bad, and then two more buildings come up at you through the trees, and two more, and two more. And they have bars on the windows, and sometimes you can hear a person screaming in there."

"Don't make a melodrama out of it, Emily," Howard said. "The first thing to do is call the hospital and find out what she was admitted for."

"It's eleven o'clock at night. Besides, they'd never tell me —a strange voice on the phone. They must have rules about that. You'd have to be a doctor to—"

"Or a lawyer, maybe," he said. "Sometimes being a lawyer comes in handy. I'll find out what her diagnosis is tomorrow, and I'll tell you tomorrow night. Okay? Now come on to bed and stop acting like an actress."

When he came home the following night he said " 'Acute alcoholism.' " Then he said "Oh, come on, Emily, that's not so bad. All she has to do is dry out and they'll let her go. It isn't as if it were 'paranoid schizophrenia,' or something like that."

That was a Monday. It was Saturday before Emily was free to ride the train out to Central Islip bringing two cartons of cigarettes (one for her sister and one for her mother); on the platform she nodded to one of the scruffy-looking cab drivers who clamored around her—they seemed to make a nice business out of one-dollar fares to the hospital and back—and then she was in that bewildering maze of trees and buildings.

Sarah's building was one of the older ones—it had a turn-of-the-century look—and Emily found her on a heavily screened upstairs verandah, sitting deep in conversation with another woman of about her own age. They both wore printed housecoats and cotton slippers, and the whole of Sarah's scalp was wrapped in something white that looked at first like a turban—the kind that had been stylish in the early forties—but proved to be a bandage.

"Emmy!" she cried. "Mary Ann, I want you to meet my brilliant sister—the one I was just telling you about. Emmy, this is my very best friend, Mary Ann Polchek."

And Emily smiled at a faded, frightened little face.

"Let's sit over here where we can talk," Sarah said, moving slowly as she led Emily to a couple of vacant chairs in the afternoon shadows. "*Gee*, it's nice of you to come all the way out here. Oh, and you've brought cigarettes, too; aren't you sweet."

"You mean that lady's your best friend from home?" Emily asked when they were settled. "Or just here?"

"Just here. She's a wonderful person. You really shouldn't

have made this long trip, dear; I'll be getting out of here in a couple of weeks."

"You will?"

"Well, three weeks at the most, my doctor says. I just needed a little rest. Actually, all I care about is getting out before the first, when Tony Junior comes home. Did I tell you his medical discharge came through?" Tony Junior had injured his hip in a jeep accident, which kept him away from Vietnam; the other recent news about him was that he was married to a California girl. "I can't wait to see him," Sarah said. "He's decided to settle in St. Charles with his family."

"His family?"

"Well, the girl he married has two children, you see."

"Oh. And what will he do?"

"Go back to work for the garage, I guess. They love him there."

"I see. Listen, Sarah, tell me about yourself. How're you feeling?"

"Fine." Sarah's smile seemed determined to prove there was nothing wrong, and Emily noticed that her teeth were white: she must have had them repaired and cleaned.

One important question had to be asked, in spite of the smile, and Emily asked it. "How did you hurt your head?"

"Oh, that was just stupid," Sarah said. "*All* my own fault. One night I got up in the middle of the night because I couldn't sleep, and I went downstairs to get a glass of milk. And on the way back I was *al*most to the top of the stairs when I slipped and fell all the way down. Wasn't that stupid?"

And Emily felt her own mouth spread in what she guessed might pass for a smile of agreement on how stupid it was. "Were you badly hurt?"

"No, no, it was nothing." Sarah vaguely indicated the head bandage with one hand. "This is nothing."

It wasn't nothing; they must have had to shave her head before the bandage went on—it was that closely wrapped —and Emily almost said Did they shave your head? but thought better of it. "Well," she said instead. "It's good to see you looking so well."

For a while they just sat smoking, smiling whenever they met each other's eyes to show that everything was all right. Sarah didn't know that Emily knew of the "acute alcoholism" diagnosis; Emily wondered if there might be any tactful way to bring it up, and decided there wasn't. It became clear as they sat there that Sarah would keep her troubles to herself from now on. There would be no more confidences now, no more telephone calls and no more requests for help.

"Do you—think things'll be all right when you go home?" Emily said.

"How do you mean?"

"You think you still might want to come to New York?"

"*Oh*, no." Sarah looked embarrassed. "That was just silly. I'm sorry I called you that night. I was just—you know— tired and upset. Those things pass. I needed a good rest, that's all."

"Because I *have* been following the 'Help Wanted' ads," Emily said, "and I have a friend who thinks you might find something at National Carbon. And there's no reason why you couldn't stay at my place for a while, until you get settled."

Sarah was shaking her head. "No, Emmy. All that's past now. Let's just forget it, okay?"

"Okay. Except that I—well, okay."

"Are you going to visit Pookie while you're here?"

"I thought I would, yes. Do you know how to get to her building?" And Emily instantly realized what a foolish question that was. How could Sarah know the location of any other building when she was locked into this one? "It doesn't matter," she said quickly. "I'll find it."

"Well," Sarah said, getting slowly to her feet. "I guess you'd better be on your way. Thanks *so* much for coming, dear; it was wonderful to see you. Give my love to Pookie."

Out under the trees again, Emily walked a long way before realizing that she couldn't remember whether the man at the door had said three buildings down and four to the right or four buildings down and three to the right, and there was no one else to ask. A sign at one intersection said E-4 to E-9, which was no help, and another sign beneath it said MORGUE. In the distance, twin smokestacks rose against the gray sky. It was probably only the power plant —she knew that—but she wondered if it might be a crematory.

"Excuse me, sir," she said to an old man sitting on a bench. "Can you tell me where—"

"Don't mess with me, lady," he said, and then, placing his thumb against one nostril, he leaned forward and blew a bright stream of snot out of the other. "Don't mess with me."

She kept walking, trying not to think of the old man, until a taxicab slowed down at the curb and the driver stuck his head out and said "Taxi?"

"Yes," she said. "Thank you."

And it really didn't matter, she assured herself as the cab pulled away toward the train station. Old Pookie would only have lain silent with a look of terminal petulance on her face; she would have extended one hand to receive the cigarettes but wouldn't have smiled, wouldn't have talked, probably wouldn't have given any sign that she knew who Emily was.

Back in the city, she waited well over three weeks before calling St. Charles to find out if Sarah was home. She did it from the office, late on a weekday morning, so that Tony wouldn't be there.

"... Oh, hi, Emmy ... Oh, sure, I've been home for days ... How's who?"

"I said how's everything?"

"Everything's fine. Tony Junior's here, with his wife and her children, so the place is something of a madhouse. She's very nice and very pregnant. They're staying here for a while, and we're helping them find a house of their own."

"I see. Well, be sure to keep in touch, Sarah. Let me know if there's anything I can—you know—anything I can do."

And Sarah did keep in touch, though not by telephone. Some time later she sent Emily a letter. The envelope was addressed in the old pert, debutantish handwriting, but the letter itself was typed, with a good many corrections marked in ballpoint pen.

Dear Emmy:

I am writing you instead of calling because I want to try out the typewriter Peter gave me for my birthday. It is an Underwood portable, second-hand, and it has a few faults here and there, but it types! With a little cleaning and readjustment, I'll be wearing it like a glove in no time.

It's a boy! Eight pounds seven ounces. And he looks just like his grandfather, my husband. (This makes my husband very angry, because it makes him tend to feel like a grandfather, and he doesn't care for the idea.) I have just finished building a bassinette. Never again! I began with a large clothes basket, some foam rubber, some padded plastic-coated fabric, some sheeting, some thumbtacks, and endless yards of blue ribbon. It was a brave beginning, and eventually a week later it reached fruition. Triumphant, but exhausted, I drove it down to Tony Junior's house, but nobody was home. The darned thing rode around in my station wagon for two days before it finally came to roost.

I am up to my ears in blackberries this week. Our pasture contains a full quarter acre of huge berries just screaming to be picked. So far I have picked, washed, syruped and frozen 30 pints, and made 20 jars of jelly, and I still can't keep ahead of them. Personally, I hate blackberries. I do this, remembering what the man said when asked why he wanted to climb Mt. Everest—"Because it's there."

I have not been to see Pookie for two very valid reasons. First, my driving is limited to strictly local stuff, at least until I gain a little more self-confidence and grow a little more hair. And second, because I almost never have the use of a car. Tony drives his T-bird to Magnum, Eric drives *his* T-bird to the motorcycle shop where he works, and Peter drives my station wagon to his summer job in Setauket.

Must say goodbye now and beat-feet back to the blackberry patch. Take care of yourself.

Love,
Sarah

"What do you make of it?" Emily asked Howard when he'd read the letter.

"What do you mean, 'make of it'? Just a cheerful little letter, that's all."

"But that's the point, Howard—it's *too* cheerful. Except for that one reference to growing her hair you'd think she was the happiest, most contented little housewife in the world."

"Maybe that's the way she likes to see herself."

"Well, but the thing is I know better—and she *knows* I know better."

"Oh, come on," Howard said, getting up from his chair to move impatiently around the room. "What do you *want* from her? You want her opening her heart to you every five minutes? Telling you how many times he's beaten her this month? When she *does* that, you say you 'don't want her dragging down your life.' You're a funny girl, Emily."

And much later that night, as they lay drained of passion in her bed, she hesitantly touched his arm and said "Howard?"

"Mm?"

"If I ask you something, will you promise to tell me the truth?"

"Mm."

"Do you really think I'm a funny girl?"

In the summer of 1967 they spent their vacations at Howard's old place in East Hampton, where he hadn't been since the final year of his marriage. She liked the brightness and the roominess and the sandy, grassy smell of the house—after the city it was like breathing pure oxygen—and she liked its weathered cedar shingles, which shone almost silver in the sun. The word "delightful" kept occurring to her ("We had a delightful time," she would say to anyone who asked, when they got back to New York). She liked the surf, and the way Howard would wade out into it and jump with each breaking wave; she liked the way his prick would shrivel up and turn purple and blue from wind and water, so that only her lips and tongue, tasting salt, could restore it to weight.

"Howard?" she said on their final morning, which was Sunday. "I was thinking I might call my sister. Maybe we could sort of make a detour and stop off to see her on our way home."

"Sure," he said. "Nice idea."

"But I mean are you sure you don't mind? It's really 'way out of our way, and we'll probably just stumble into some dreadful, squalid scene."

"Christ's sake, Emily, of course I don't mind. I've always wanted to meet your sister."

And so she made the call. A man answered, but it wasn't Tony. "She's resting now," he said. "Can I take a message?"

"Well, no, I just—who's this? Is this Tony Junior?"

"No, it's Peter."

"Oh, *Peter*. Well, I just—this is Emily. Emily Grimes."

"Aunt Emmy!" he said. "I *thought* that sounded like your voice . . ."

It was arranged that they would stop by between two and three o'clock that afternoon. "You'd better brace yourself, Howard," she said when they'd found their way into St. Charles at last. "This'll be perfectly awful."

"Don't be silly," he told her.

She had hoped Peter might answer the door—then there would be an embrace and a courteous handshake ("How do you do, sir?") before they moved laughing into the living room—but instead it was Tony. He opened the door only a few inches and stood ready to slam it, like a man intent on protecting the sanctity of his home. When he saw who it was he blinked and stepped back, opening it wider, and Emily wondered how she could possibly greet him, after calling him a bastard and a son of a bitch and threatening his life. "Hello, Tony," she said. "This is Howard Dunninger; Tony Wilson."

He moved his mouth a little to mumble that he was pleased to meet Howard, and ushered them through the vestibule.

Sarah sat curled up on the sofa, the way old Edna Wilson used to sit, smiling vaguely. Emily looked into that smile for at least a second before realizing what was wrong with it: the lower half of Sarah's face was collapsed.

"Oh, Emmy," she wailed, trying ineffectually to hide her mouth with one hand, "I forgot to put my *teef* in."

"That's all right," Emily said. "Sit still." But it was clear that Sarah had been sitting still all day; she might not have been able to get up if she'd wanted to.

"Come sit beside me, Emmy," she said when the introductions were over. "It's so wonderful to *see* you." And she took both of Emily's hands in a surprisingly strong grip. Emily found it awkward to sit there, reaching sideways to allow her hands to be squeezed and fondled in her sister's lap; the only thing to do was move in closer, until their thighs touched, and when she did that she came into the zone of a heavy, fruity smell of alcohol.

". . . My very own baby sister," Sarah was saying while Emily tried not to look at her dark, grinning gums. "Do all you people realize this is my very own baby sister?"

Tony sat stolidly in a chair across from the sofa, wearing paint-stained dungarees and looking like an exhausted laborer. Beside him, Howard Dunninger smiled uneasily. The only self-assured member of the group was Peter, who had turned into a striking young man. He was dressed in spattered work clothes too—he and his father had been painting the house before their guests arrived—and Emily liked his looks. He wasn't tall and he wasn't quite handsome, but he moved around in a graceful way and there was something humorous and wise about his face.

"Have you finished at the seminary yet, Peter?" she asked him.

"One more year to go," he said. "It starts next week."

"How was your summer?"

"Oh, okay, thanks. I was in Africa for a while."

"In Africa? Really?"

And he held the floor for a few minutes, mercifully saving everyone else from conversational effort, while he described Africa as a sleeping giant "just beginning to stretch." When he said that he raised and spread both shapely arms, fists clenched, in a sleepy stretching motion, and it occurred to Emily that there must be any number of young girls who thought Peter Wilson was a dreamboat.

"Oh, Emmy," Sarah said. "My brilliant little baby sister —I love you."

"Well," Emily said. "That's nice." And she realized at once, if only because Tony was looking at her narrowly, that it had been the wrong thing to say. "I mean," she amended, "*you* know; I love you too."

"Isn't she marvelous?" Sarah asked the company. "Isn't my little sister marvelous? What do you think, Howie? Is it all right to call you Howie?"

"Sure," Howard said kindly. "I think she's marvelous."

It had been over a year now since Sarah's head was shaved, but her hair still had a cropped, untidy look, and it was lusterless. The rest of her, beneath that half-collapsed face, was all sag and bloat: she looked a great deal older than her age. Soon the others began to talk among themselves, leaving the sisters alone on the sofa, and Emily used the opportunity to say "I didn't know you'd lost your teeth, Sarah. When did that happen?"

"Oh, I don't know; couple of years ago," Sarah said in the same embarrassed, pointedly offhand way she'd dismissed her head wound as "nothing" in Central Islip, and Emily realized too late that it hadn't been a very tactful question. To atone for it she squeezed the pale hands that were squeezing her own and said "You're looking very well."

"Peter!" Sarah called sharply, and Emily thought she might say "Shape up," but instead she said "Tell the story about the old Negro priest you met in Africa."

"Never mind that now, Mom," he said.

"Oh, please. Come on, Peter."

"Mom, I'd really rather not, okay? It isn't a 'story' anyway."

"Of course it is," she insisted. "When Peter was in Africa he met this wonderful old Negro priest, and he—"

"Mom, will you cut it out?" he said, smiling to show he wasn't really annoyed with her, and only then did she leave him alone. Still smiling, he puckered his lips very slightly as if to blow her a kiss. Then he turned to Howard and said "What kind of legal work do you do, sir?"

A little later the kitchen door slammed and a hulking, squint-eyed youth came in, wearing a studded leather jacket and motorcycle boots, looking as if he meant harm to them all; it took Emily a moment to realize that this was Sarah's third son, Eric. He dipped his head politely at Emily and shook hands with Howard; then he drew his father and brother aside for a long mumbled conference that seemed to be about the workings of an automobile, and when their business was concluded he slouched outdoors again.

It was a bright September afternoon. Trees stirred in the wind beyond the windows, and mottled shadows moved on the dusty floor. No one could think of anything to talk about.

"Anthony?" Sarah said quietly, as if reminding her husband of some private duty.

"Mm," he replied, and went out to the kitchen. When he came back he carried what looked like a glass of orange juice, but there was nothing festive in his way of bringing it to her: the glass hung from his fingers, close to one thigh of his jeans, and he seemed to sneak it into her waiting hand. She took the first few swallows slowly and solemnly enough to make clear that it contained vodka or gin.

"Anyone like some—coffee or something?" Tony Wilson asked his guests.

"No, thanks," Emily said. "Actually, we'd better be going; it's a long drive."

"Oh, you *can't* go," Sarah told her. "You only just *got* here. I won't *let* you go." Then, as her drink began to take effect, she brightened with a new idea. "Peter," she said. "Will you do me a favor? One little favor?"

"What's that?"

She paused for dramatic effect. "Get the guitar."

He looked mortified. "Oh, no, Mom," he said, and one of his hands, hanging from his knee as he sat, made a little negative gesture to show it was out of the question.

"Please, Peter."

"No."

But Sarah wouldn't take no for an answer. "All you have to do," she explained, "is go out to your car and get it, and bring it back in here, and play 'Where Have All the Flowers Gone.'"

In the end it was Tony who broke the deadlock. "He doesn't want to, dear," he told his wife.

Then Emily got to her feet, smiling, to prove she'd meant it when she'd said that she and Howard had better be going.

Sarah, looking bewildered on the sofa, did not get up to wish them goodbye.

There were no more letters from Sarah, and no telephone calls. At Christmastime the Wilsons' card was signed hastily by Tony, rather than in Sarah's jubilant hand, and this was briefly disturbing.

"Do you think I ought to call her?" Emily asked Howard.

"What for? Just because of the Christmas card? No, honey. If she's in any kind of trouble she'll call you."

"Okay. I suppose you're right."

And then late one night in May of 1968—three months, as Emily figured out later, before Sarah's forty-seventh birthday—the ringing phone brought Emily stumbling out of bed.

"Aunt Emily?"

"Peter?"

"No, it's Tony—Tony Junior . . . I'm afraid your sister passed away today."

And the first thing that occurred to her, even before the news sank in, was that it was just like Tony Junior to have said "passed away" instead of "died."

"What did she—die of?" she inquired after a moment.

"She'd been suffering from a liver ailment for a long time," he said huskily, "so it was mostly that, complicated by a fall she took in the house."

"I see." And Emily heard her own voice sink to the hushed solemnity with which people receive the news of death in the movies. None of this seemed real. "How's your father taking it?"

"Oh, he's—holding up pretty well."

"Well," she said, "give him my—you know—give him my love."

CHAPTER 2

Howard's car was being repaired, so they had to go out to the funeral on the train.

"Change a jamake," the conductor told them.

All the way to St. Charles, staring through a dirty window at the slowly wheeling suburbs, Emily gave herself over to memories of her sister. Sarah at twenty, elegantly dressed in borrowed clothes and complaining that she didn't care about the silly Easter parade; Sarah at sixteen with braces on her teeth, bending over the sink each night to wash her sweaters; Sarah at twelve; Sarah at nine.

At nine or ten, Sarah had been much the more imaginative of the girls. She could take a ten-cent book of Woolworth paper dolls, cut out the dolls and their tabbed clothing without ever going over the lines, and invest each dressed doll with a personality of its own. She would decide which of the girl dolls was the prettiest and most popular (and if she felt her dress wasn't nice enough she would design and make a better one, using crayons or watercolor paints); then she would fold all the other dolls forward at the hips to make them sit down as an audience; she would hold the performer upright, make her tremble very slightly the way real singers do, and have her sing "Welcome, Sweet Springtime" or "Look for the Silver Lining," to both of which she knew all the words.

"You okay, Emily?" Howard asked, touching her arm.

"Sure," she said. "I'm fine."

Young Eric met them at the station, wearing mirror sunglasses and dressed in a cheap dark suit from which his big wrists hung like slabs of meat.

"Is Peter here yet?" she asked him.

"Everybody's here," he said as he steered them expertly through traffic.

This was going to be awful. The only thing to do was get through it, get it over with somehow, and try to remember that Howard Dunninger was there with her. He rode alone in the back seat of Eric's car, but by turning her head very slightly she could see the well-pressed Oxford-gray flannel of his trousers, and that was comforting.

"There isn't gonna be a real funeral," Eric said at the wheel. "We're just gonna have a little service at the—you know—at the graveside."

Then they were all walking on fresh grass among tombstones, under a blue sky, and it occurred to Emily that the Wilsons must really have been an important family after all, if they had a private burial plot in one of the most crowded sections of Long Island. Sarah's open grave was covered with a gray tarpaulin. Her closed coffin, lying on the contraption that would lower it into the earth, looked quite small—she had never been very big except in child-hood memories. Not far away, one of the newer-looking tombstones read "Edna; beloved wife of Geoffrey," and that was the first Emily knew that old Edna had died: it was funny Sarah hadn't told her. She made a mental note to ask Sarah about it after the ceremony, before it struck her that she could never ask Sarah anything again. Very shyly, like a child seeking her father's forgiveness, she put her fingers through Howard's arm. She could almost hear Sarah's voice saying "It's okay, Emmy. It's okay."

To their left a big, soft-looking man stood weeping, or rather working his lips in an effort at self-control and blink-ing his red eyes; close beside him was a matronly young woman with a toddling infant and an older boy and girl clinging to her skirt. It was Tony Junior with his wife and baby and stepchildren. The minister was there too, clasp-ing his small prayer book while they waited for the other mourners to arrive.

Several car doors slammed in the distance and soon a cluster of men appeared, walking quickly. Tony was in the middle, in animated conversation with another man. He seemed to be laughing and talking at the same time, and he repeatedly made the same gesture he had used years ago in telling Jack Flanders about the takeoff speed of Magnum jet fighters ("Shoom!")—knifing the flat of his hand straight ahead from his temple. The man beside him smiled and nodded, and once he cuffed Tony's shoulder with his fist. From their clothes and bearing—starchy and solid, lower middle class—Emily assumed that these other men were some of Tony's co-workers at the Magnum plant; behind them came Peter and another group, solemn young men of about his own age who looked like graduate students.

Tony was still talking when he came up to where Emily and Howard stood. "... Straight ahead, right?" he demanded of the man beside him. "No looking back"—he made the hand-and-temple gesture—"everything straight ahead."

"Right, Tony," the man said. "That's it."

"Oh, I say," Tony said, blinking. "Hello, Emmy." The hollows of his eyes were red and swollen, as if he'd vigorously ground his fists into them for a long time.

"Hello, Tony."

Then he saw Howard and shook hands with him. "Nice to see you, Mr. Howinger. I say, one of our men went over to your firm last month; I told him 'I know the *legal* counsel there; might be useful for you.' P'raps you'll run into him; hell of a nice chap named—or no, wait. That was Union Carbide."

"Well," Howard said, "they're pretty much the same thing."

And Tony turned his inflamed eyes on Emily again. He seemed to be trying to tell her something for which he lacked the words. "I say," he said, bringing the flat of his hand up beside one eye. "Straight ahead. No looking back; no looking sideways—" The hand shot forward. "Straight ahead."

"Right, Tony," she said.

When the ceremony began the Magnum men and the graduate students stood back at a respectful distance. Peter, whose eyes and mouth looked free of any emotion but concern, led his father off to one side of the grave and held him firmly by the upper arm as if to keep him from falling. As the minister's voice intoned the ecclesiastical words Tony's jaws fell open and several strands of spittle clung and trembled between his lips.

"... Earth to earth," the minister was saying, "ashes to ashes, dust to dust ..." and he crumbled a handful of dirt on the top of Sarah's coffin to symbolize her burial.

Then it was over, and they were all walking out of the cemetery. Peter had turned his father over to the Magnum men; now he fell into step with Emily and Howard and said "You're coming back to the house with us for a while, aren't you? Here, we'll go in my car."

Except that his hands shook a little on the ignition key and the steering wheel, he seemed wholly in control of himself. "Those younger guys are friends of mine from the seminary," he said as he drove. "I didn't ask them to come; they found out about it and came out on their own. It always surprises me how kind people are."

"Mm," Emily said. She wanted to say How did she die, Peter? Tell me the truth; instead she turned her head to watch the bright supermarkets and filling stations slide past. "Peter," she said after a while. "Is your grandfather well?"

"Oh, he's fine, Aunt Emmy. He wanted to come out today, but he didn't feel up to it. He's been in a nursing home for some time, you see."

The old house looked even more gaunt and forbidding than Emily had remembered it. One of Tony Junior's stepchildren opened the door for them, giggled, and ran away to hide in the musty living room; the rest of the party was assembled around the dining-room table, which was strewn with sandwich makings and with bottles of beer and soda. It was a noisy gathering.

"... And *this* guy," one of the Magnum men was saying, punching Tony heartily on the shoulder, "this guy catches one measly little blowfish, and he makes such a big deal out of it I thought he's gonna tip the *boat* over."

Tony, his eyes still swollen, rolled with the punch in a spasm of laughter and raised a can of beer to his lips.

"Can I get you something, Aunt Emmy?" Peter asked.

"No, thanks. Well, yes—I'll take a beer, if you have enough."

"You, sir?"

"Nothing for now, thanks," Howard said. "I'm fine."

"No, but I'll never forget this *one* time we went out," the man from Magnum said. Flushed with the success of his first fishing story, he launched into another without seeming to notice that he'd lost most of his audience. "Who-all was with us that time, Tony? You, me, Fred Slovick—I forget. Anyway, we . . ."

"Anybody else on the liverwurst?" Tony Junior inquired. He was taking sandwich orders. "You want the regular mustard on that, or the baby-shit?" His wife, who had apparently put the baby down for a nap, was trying to wipe spilled Coca-Cola from the dress of a peevish five-year-old.

"Tell me one thing, though." One of the seminary students, a pleasant-looking boy with a Southern accent, directed a shy smile at Tony Junior. "One thing I don't understand. How come you didn't beat up on your brother more when you were kids?"

"Oh, I tried," Tony Junior said, spreading mayonnaise on rye bread. "I tried plenty of times, but it wasn't easy. I mean he's little, but he's wiry."

". . . So I says 'I got five bucks,' " the Magnum man was shouting. " 'I got *five bucks* says Wilson don't catch nothin' all day.' "

"Ah, Christ, Marty," Tony said, laughing and shaking his head in happy exasperation, "You'll be telling that story when we're *all* dead."

Peter went to answer the phone; when he came back he said "It's for you, Dad."

Still glowing in the aftermath of Marty's story (of which the punch line was that he'd caught more blowfish than anyone else in the boat that day), Tony narrowed his eyes over a shot glass of whiskey and said "Who is it, Pete?"

"It's Sergeant Ryan. You know; over at the station."

Tony knocked back his whiskey and grimaced at the sweet pain of its taste. "Police," he muttered, getting to his feet. "Damned police think I killed my wife."

"Oh, now, Dad, come on," Peter said in a mollifying way as he followed his father out of the room. "You know better than that. I've told you and told you, it's only a routine investigation."

Tony's talk with Sergeant Ryan didn't last long; when he rejoined the party he had another drink—two bottles of whiskey were being passed around the table now—and the shouts and laughter went on far into the late afternoon.

Dark blue shadows filled the house when Emily got up to make her way to the bathroom. In the hallway she stumbled and nearly fell; righting herself, she found she had collided with a small cabinet bearing old copies of the *Daily News* stacked three feet high. On the way back she passed a framed photograph, the picture of Tony and Sarah on Easter Sunday of 1941. It was hanging awry, as if from the impact of some heavy blow that had shuddered the wall. Carefully, with unsteady fingers, she reached up and straightened it.

Lights were being turned on against the heavily gathering dusk.

". . . No, but what *I* want to know," the Magnum man was saying to Tony Junior, "what *I* want to know is what kind of a job you guys can do for me."

"The best, Marty," Tony Junior assured him. "You can ask anybody: we're the best mechanics in this part of Suffolk County."

"Because I mean from *my* standpoint of view," Marty persisted, "from *my* standpoint of view that's the only—you know—the only consideration."

"Ma," one of the children whined. "Hey, Ma, c'we go home now?"

"I say, come and have a drink," Tony said to a hesitant group of seminary students. "Don't you chaps ever drink?"

"Thank you, sir," one of them said. "A little bourbon and water."

"Are you all right, Emily?" Howard inquired, looking up from his conversation with another of the Magnum men.

"I'm fine. Can I get you a drink?"

"I've got one, thanks."

Through it all Eric stood leaning alone against the kitchen doorjamb, silent and inscrutable behind his mirror sunglasses, like a young security guard hired to keep the party from getting out of hand.

Tony Junior's wife took the children home without saying goodbye to anyone; not long after that the seminary students left, and then all the Magnum men but Marty made their departure.

". . . Listen, Tony," Marty said. "You gotta eat, right? Let's everybody go grab a steak at Manny's."

And in several cars, after some drink-fuddled preliminary bickering about who would ride with whom, the mourners roared down the highway to a floodlit California-style restaurant called Manny Feldon's Chop House.

It was so dark inside the place that they could scarcely see across the table as they raised their heavy cocktail glasses. Peter was sober: he sat close beside his father, as if this ceremony too, like the one in the graveyard, might require his assistance. Marty and Tony Junior were once again deep in their talk of business, though now it seemed to have taken a philosophical turn. There was no substitute for honest workmanship in any field, Marty was saying, while Tony Junior nodded slowly and steadily to show he couldn't agree more. "I mean *any* field, whether it's mechanics or carpentry or shoemaking or you name it. Am I right?"

Emily held her edge of the table firmly in both hands because it had become the only steady surface in sight: everything else was shifting and turning. Beside her in the deep upholstery against the wall—and the wall was unsteady too—Howard was putting away enough liquor to suggest that this might be the third or fourth night since she'd known him that he would go to bed drunk.

Eric sat close to no one, and he was the only one who ate heartily when the giant steaks arrived. He ate with the rhythmic passion of a starving man, hunched over his plate as if to guarantee that it wouldn't be snatched away.

". . . No, but the older I get," Marty was saying "—and mind you, I figure I've only got maybe fifteen years tops—the older I get the more I stop and think. I mean you see these kids today running around with their long hair and their crummy jeans and their crazy ideas, and what do *they* know? Am I right? I mean what do *they* know?"

In the end Howard proved sober enough to fish the timetable out of his pocket, study it in the wavering glow of his cigarette lighter and determine that they had fifteen minutes to catch the last train.

"Keep in touch, Aunt Emmy," Peter said, rising to wish

them goodbye, and he shook hands with Howard. "Thanks for coming out, sir."

Tony struggled out of his chair, swaying. He mumbled something inaudible to Howard, wiped his mouth and looked undecided about whether to give Emily a kiss on the cheek. Instead he held her hand for a second, not quite looking her in the eyes; then he let go, brought his own hand slowly up to his temple and shot it forward. "Straight ahead," he said.

It took Emily a long time to realize that Sarah was dead. Sometimes, waking from a dream of childhood filled with Sarah's face and Sarah's voice, she would go and study her own face in the bright bathroom mirror until she found assurance that it was still the face of Sarah's sister, and that it didn't look old.

"Howard?" she said once when they were lying in bed, waiting for sleep. "Do you know something? I really wish you could have known Sarah in the old days, before everything went to pieces. She was lovely."

"Mm," he said.

"Lovely and bright and full of life—and this may sound silly, but I think if you'd known her then it might've helped you to know me better."

"Oh, I don't know. I think I know you pretty well."

"No you don't," she said.

"Mm?"

"You don't really. We hardly ever talk."

"Are you kidding? We talk all the damn time, Emily."

"You never want to hear about my childhood or anything."

"Sure I do. I know all about your childhood. Besides, everybody's childhood is pretty much alike."

"How can you *say* that? Only the most obtuse, insensitive person in the *world* could say a thing like that."

"Okay, okay, okay," he said sleepily. "Tell me a story about your childhood. Make it heartbreaking."

"*Ugh!*" And she rolled away from him. "You're impossible. You're a Neanderthal."

"Mm."

Another time, when they were coming back from a drive in the country at dusk, she said "How can you be so sure it was cirrhosis, Howard?"

"I'm not sure; I just said it was most likely, considering the way she drank."

"But then there's that fishy business of the 'fall she took in the house.' And the police calling up, and Tony saying 'The police think I killed my wife.' I'll bet he did, Howard. I'll bet he flew into a drunken rage and hit her with a chair or something."

"They didn't arrest him, did they? If they'd had any evidence they'd have arrested him."

"Well, but he and the boys could've *concealed* the evidence."

"Honey, we've been over all this a hundred times. It's just one of those things you'll never know. Life is full of things like that."

Three or four old barns went by, and then any number of suburban developments, and then the beginnings of the Bronx; they were all the way to the Henry Hudson Bridge before she said "You're right."

"Right about what?"

"Life *is* full of things like that."

There were things she would never know about Howard, too, however much she might love him. Sometimes it seemed that she scarcely knew him at all.

* * *

Things weren't going very well at work. Hannah Baldwin seldom asked Emily out to lunch any more—she had
taken to having lunch with one of the younger women in
Emily's department—and she seldom called her "honey,"
nor did she often come out of her private office to place
one stout, well-clad haunch on the edge of Emily's desk
and waste whole hours with idle chatter in the middle of
a working day. She had begun to give her what Emily
described to Howard as "funny looks"—speculative, not
very friendly looks—and she found things to criticize in
the way Emily did her job.

"This copy's flat," she said once of something on which
Emily had worked for many days. "It just lies there. Isn't
there some way you can breathe a little life into it?"

When the name of a Swedish importer came out in print
without the umlaut over one of its vowels, Hannah heavily
implied that it was all Emily's fault. And when Emily let
a National Carbon ad go through production without
noticing that the words "patent pending" did not appear
after "Tynol," Hannah behaved as if it were a calamity.
"Have you any idea what the *legal* implications are in a
thing like this?" she demanded.

"Hannah, I'm sure it'll be all right," Emily said. "I
know the legal counsel for National Carbon."

Hannah blinked and squinted. "You 'know' him? What
do you mean, you 'know' him?"

Emily felt blood in her face. "I mean we're friends."

There was a pause. "Well," Hannah said at last, "it's nice
to have friends, but it doesn't have much to do with the
business world."

That night Emily told Howard about it, at dinner, and
he said "Sounds to me like she's going through menopause.

Not a hell of a lot you can do about that." He sliced off a piece of steak and chewed it thoroughly before swallowing. Then he said "Why don't you quit the damn job, Emily? You don't have to work. We don't need the money."

"No, no," she said quickly. "It's not that bad; I'm not ready to do anything like that." But later, standing at the sink to wash the dishes while he fixed himself an after-dinner drink, she felt a powerful urge to cry. She wanted to go to him and weep attractively against his shirt. He had said "We don't need the money," just as if they were married.

One evening, a year after Sarah's death, a tired woman's voice identifying itself as Central Islip State Hospital called up to say "We regret to inform you of the death of Esther Grimes."

"Oh," Emily said. "I see. Well, can you tell me what the procedure is?"

"The procedure?"

"I mean—you know—about funeral arrangements."

"That's entirely up to you, Miss Grimes."

"I know it's up to me. All I mean is—"

"If you wish a private funeral, we can recommend several funeral homes in this area."

"Just recommend one, okay?"

"My instructions are to recommend several."

"Oh. Well, okay, wait—let me get a pencil." And as she passed Howard's chair on her way from the phone she said "My mother's dead. Whaddya know about that?"

When her business was concluded Howard said "Emily? Would you like me to go along with you out there to-morrow?"

"Oh, no," she told him. "It'll just be an awful little ceremony at the whaddyacallit, the mortuary. I can handle it myself."

All three of Pookie's grandsons were waiting under the Central Islip trees when Emily's taxi pulled up outside the mortuary the next afternoon. They were the only people there. Peter left his brothers and came forward to help her out of the cab, smiling. "Good to see you, Aunt Emmy," he said. He was wearing a clerical collar; he had been ordained. "Normally they send a priest over from the hospital to perform these services," he said, "but I asked if I could do it and they said okay."

"Well, that's—that's fine, Peter," she said. "That's very nice."

The dim chapel smelled of dust and varnish. Emily, Eric and Tony Junior sat in the front pew, facing the altar where Pookie's closed coffin lay between two candlesticks. Then Peter came in through a side door, wearing some kind of Episcopalian stole, and began to read aloud from his prayer book.

". . . We brought nothing into this world, and it is certain we can take nothing out. The Lord gave, and the Lord hath taken away; blessed be the name of the Lord . . ."

When it was over, Emily went out to the office and up to a cashier's window, where a man gave her an itemized invoice and accepted her check in payment, after asking to see her driver's license. "You may accompany the remains to the crematory," he said, "but I wouldn't recommend it. There's nothing to see."

"Thank you," she said, remembering the twin smokestacks on the Central Islip horizon.

"Thank *you*."

The three Wilson boys were waiting for her. "Aunt

Emmy?" Peter said. "I know my father'd like to see you. Can I drive you over there, just for a few minutes?"

"Well, I—all right, sure."

"How about you guys?"

But it turned out that both his brothers had to get back to their jobs, and after they'd mumbled goodbye their cars roared away in different directions.

"My father's married again," Peter said as he drove her down a long straight road. "Did you know that?"

"No; no, I didn't."

"Best thing in the world for him. He married a very nice lady who owns a restaurant in St. Charles, a widow. They'd been friends for years."

"I see. And do they live in the old—"

"Oh, no; Great Hedges is long gone. He sold it to a developer soon after my mother died. There's nothing out there now but dirt and bulldozers. No, he moved in with his new wife—her name's Vera—in an apartment over the restaurant. It's very nice. And he's retired from Magnum— did you know that?"

"No."

"Well, he was in a bad car accident about six months ago, suffered a bad head injury and broke his shoulder, so he took his retirement early. Now he's just sort of recuperating and taking things easy; I imagine when he's ready to work again he'll go partners with Vera in the restaurant business."

"I see." After a while it occurred to her to ask about old Geoffrey. "How's your grandfather, Peter?"

"Oh, he died, Aunt Emmy. He died last year."

"Well, I'm—very sorry to hear that."

The fields on either side of the road gave way to dense masses of houses, and to shopping centers with acres of parked cars. "Tell me about yourself, Peter," she said. "Where are you located now?"

"I lucked into a terrific job," he said, glancing briefly away from the wheel. "I'm assistant chaplain at Edwards College, up in New Hampshire. Have you heard of Edwards?"

"Certainly."

"I couldn't have asked for a better situation in a first job," he went on. "My boss is a fine man, a fine priest, and we seem to think alike. The work is very challenging and very gratifying. Besides, I like working with young people."

"Mm," she said. "Well, that's fine. Congratulations."

"What about you, Aunt Emmy?"

"Oh, things are pretty much the same with me."

There was a long pause. Then, staring meditatively at the road ahead, he said "You know something? I've always admired you, Aunt Emmy. My mother used to say 'Emmy's a free spirit.' I didn't know what that meant when I was little, so I asked her once. And she said 'Emmy doesn't care what anybody thinks. She's her own person and she goes her own way.'"

The walls of Emily's throat closed up. When she felt it was safe to speak she said "Did she really say that?"

"As nearly as I can remember, that's exactly what she said."

They were traveling now through suburban streets so thickly populated that he had to keep braking for stoplights. "It's not much farther," he said. "Right around this next corner . . . Here."

The restaurant's sign promised STEAK and LOBSTERS and COCKTAILS, but it had a dreary look: the paint was flaking off its white clapboard front, and its windows were too small. It was the kind of place that a hungry man and woman in a car might spend several minutes considering ("Whaddya think?" "Well, I don't know; it looks sort of awful. Maybe there'll be a better place further on." "Honey, I've told you: there won't be anything else for miles." "Oh, well, in that case—sure; what the hell.")

Peter parked in the weed-grown gravel of its parking lot and led Emily around behind the building to a wooden staircase that led up to a second-story door.

"Dad?" he called. "You home?"

And there was Tony Wilson, looking like an aging, bewildered Laurence Olivier as he opened the flimsy door and let them in. "I say," he said. "Hello, Emmy."

The small apartment had a makeshift look—it reminded Emily of Pookie's old apartment over the garage at Great Hedges—and it contained too much furniture. Two of Tony's ancestors stared from the cluttered walls; the other pictures were the kind that come with picture frames purchased in a five- and ten-cent store. Vera came bustling in from the kitchen, all smiles, a vigorous big-boned woman in her forties, wearing shorts.

"I hope you won't think my legs are always this heavy," she said. "I have these terrible allergies, and sometimes they make my legs swell up." And she struck her fist against one quivering thigh to indicate the excess flesh. "Can you find a place to sit down? Peter, move that box out of the blue chair so she can sit down."

"Thank you," Emily said.

"We were so sorry to hear about your mother," Vera said in a lowered voice, sitting beside Tony on a small sofa that Emily recognized from the old house. "You only get one mother."

"Well, she'd been—very sick for a long time."

"I know. My mother went the same way. Five years in

and out of the hospital, in constant pain. Cancer of the pancreas. My first husband, too—cancer of the colon. He died in agony. And *this* one." She nudged Tony heavily in the upper arm. "*God*, what a scare he gave me. Did Peter tell you about the accident? Oh, I forgot to offer you something. Would you care for some coffee? Or some tea?"

"No, thanks; neither one. I'm fine."

"Have a cookie, anyway; they're good." She pointed to a plate of chocolate-chip cookies on the coffee table. Peter reached over and took one, which he munched while she went on talking. "*Any*way," she said, "the Highway Patrol called me at five-thirty in the afternoon, and I got over to the hospital before they started working on him. They had him lying on a stretcher in the emergency room, unconscious, blood all over the place, and I swear to God I thought he was dead. His brains were spilling out."

"Okay, Vera," Peter said around a mouthful of cookie.

She turned on him, her eyes round with innocence and indignation. "You don't believe me? You don't believe me? I swear to God. I swear to God, Peter, the man's brains were spilling out in his *hair*."

Peter swallowed. "Well," he said, "at least they managed to patch him up." And he turned to his father. "Dad, here's the piece I was telling you about, the one I thought you might like to read." From the inside pocket of his coat he drew a folded brochure, handsomely printed on rich tan paper, with an old-English kind of crest and the words "Edwards College" as part of its heading.

"What's this?" Vera demanded, still bridling over his disbelief of the brains in the hair. "A sermon or something?"

"Oh, come on, Vera," Peter said. "You know I don't give you sermons. It's just a bulletin my church puts out."

"Mm," Tony said. He pulled a pair of reading glasses from his shirt pocket, put them on and peered through them at the brochure, blinking several times.

"That first article is by my boss," Peter explained. "You might enjoy reading that too. My own piece is on the inside page."

"Mm." Tony carefully put the brochure away in his shirt pocket, along with his glasses and his pack of cigarettes, and said "Ve'y good, Pete."

"Oh, this Peter," Vera confided to Emily. "Isn't he too much? Isn't he gonna make some girl happy one of these days?"

"He certainly is."

"Tony Junior and I have our problems," she said, "and Eric—well, I don't know about Eric; but this Peter. He really is too much. Only you know what, though? They're spoiling him, all those women up at Edwards College. Spoiling him rotten. They *feed* him; they make his *bed* for him; they take out his *laundry* for him—"

"Okay, Vera," Peter said, and then he inspected his watch. "I guess we'd better be getting started, Aunt Emmy, if we want to make that train."

Once during the following winter Howard had to go to Los Angeles again—the seventh or eighth such trip he'd made since she'd known him.

"I won't *need* all this heavy stuff," he said when she was helping him to pack. "You don't understand how warm it is out there."

"Oh," she said. "That's right, I forgot." And she let him do the rest of the packing by himself.

She went into the kitchen to make coffee, but changed her mind and fixed herself a drink instead. These departures were always upsetting. She was determined not to ask him if he intended to see Linda: the last time she'd asked him that, on his third or fourth trip, it had brought on what almost amounted to a fight. Besides, she assured herself as the alcohol warmed her blood, it wasn't really very likely. He and Linda had been separated for almost six years now—six *years*, for God's sake—and though he sometimes still talked about her in the old infuriating way, it certainly ought to be clear by now that the marriage was dissolved.

But that brought up the insidious question that had nagged her from the beginning, threatening time and again to make her fly at him with shrill and redundant demands for an answer: if the marriage was dissolved, why didn't they get a divorce?

"What's the deal?" Howard said, smiling in the kitchen doorway. "You drinking alone?"

"Sure. I always drink alone when you go on these trips. I'm getting in practice for when you disappear to California for good. Give me a few years and I'll be one of these terrible old ladies you see on the street with four shopping bags, picking through trash cans and talking to themselves."

"Cut it out, Emily. You mad at me? What're you mad about?"

"Of course I'm not 'mad' at you. Would you like a drink?"

That particular California trip gave her no cause for worry. He called her four times while he was gone, and the fourth time, when he said he was tired, she said "Listen, Howard: don't go through that awful business of taking a cab home from the airport. I'll drive the car out and meet you."

"No, no," he said. "You don't have to do that."

"I know I don't have to. It's just a thing I'd like to do."

There was a pause while he seemed to think it over. Then he said "Okay, good. You're a sweetheart, Emily."

She wasn't used to driving his big, quiet car, especially at night and in the rain. Its power and fluidity frightened her —she applied the brakes more often than necessary, causing drivers behind her to sound their horns—but she enjoyed the rich, massive feel of it and the way the dark, dark green of its broad hood was pearled with trembling raindrops.

Howard looked drawn and exhausted as he emerged from the plane ramp—he looked old—but when he caught sight of her his face glowed in a way that was almost boyish. "Damn," he said. "It sure is nice to find you waiting here."

Less than a year later he went to California again—and this time his absence was filled with silence and dread. She couldn't even plan to meet him with the car because she wasn't sure which day or night he'd come home, let alone on which flight. All she could do was wait—trying to appease Hannah Baldwin's disgruntlement through the working hours, trying to suppress a keen temptation to drink herself to sleep in the evenings.

Once during that time, walking back to the office after lunch, she saw a haggard, petulant woman's face—a face that anyone would have said was aging badly (lined and deeply shadowed eyes; a weak, self-pitying mouth)—and found with a shock that it was herself, caught unawares in the reflection of a plate-glass window. That night, alone at the bathroom mirror, she tried any number of ways to make the face look better: crinkling its eyes in a subtle smile and then in a wider smile of pure delight, tightening and loosening its lips to varying degrees, using a hand mirror to gauge the effects of its profile from different angles, experimenting tirelessly with new ways of enhancing its shape through different arrangements of her hair. Then, in front of the full-length mirror in the vestibule, she took off all her clothes and scrutinized her body under bright lights. Her belly had to be sucked flat before it looked right, but having small breasts was almost an advantage now; there wasn't much that age could do to them. Turning away, she peered over her shoulder to confirm the knowledge that her buttocks were underslung and the backs of her thighs wrinkled; but in general, she decided, facing the mirror again, she wasn't bad at all. She paced off a distance of ten feet, until she stood on the living-room carpet, and there she went through a series of the steps and positions she had learned in a modern dance class at Barnard. It was good exercise, and it gave her a proudly erotic feeling. The distant mirror showed a slim, lithe girl in effortless motion, until she put a foot wrong and froze into awkwardness. She was breathing hard and beginning to sweat. This was silly.

The thing to do was take a shower. But when she walked into the bathroom the medicine-cabinet mirror caught her as cruelly as the window on the street that day, and there it was again: the face of a middle-aged woman in hopeless and terrible need.

Howard came home two nights after the night she stopped expecting him, and she knew the moment she saw him, if not from the very sound of his key in the lock, that it was all over.

"... I would've called you," he explained, "but I didn't see any point in waking you up just to say I'd be a little late. How've you been?"

"All right. How was your trip?"

"Oh, it was—quite a trip. Let me get us both a drink, and then we'll talk." From the kitchen, over the sounds of ice cubes and glassware, he called "Actually, Emily, there's quite a lot to talk about," and he came back to her with two clicking highballs. He looked guilty. "First of all," he began after the heavy sigh that followed his first few sips, "I don't suppose it's really news to you that I've seen Linda occasionally on some of these trips over the past—however long it's been."

"No," she said. "That's not really news."

"Sometimes I'd finish work a day or two ahead of time," he went on, sounding encouraged, "and I'd fly up to San Francisco and we'd have dinner together. Nothing more than that. She'd tell me about how she was doing—and actually she's doing very well: she and another girl have their own business, designing clothes—and I'd just sit there acting sort of like her father. Once or twice I'd ask her if she'd met any nice guys, and then when she'd tell me about men she'd been 'seeing' or 'dating' I'd feel my heart start to pound like some crazy—I don't know. I'd feel the blood racing all the way down to my fingertips. I'd feel—"

"Get to the point, Howard."

"All right." He drank off nearly all of his bourbon-and-water and then he sighed again, as if in relief that the hard part was over. "The point is there wasn't really any National Carbon business on this trip," he said. "I did lie to you on that score, Emily, and I'm sorry. I hate lying. I spent the whole time with Linda. She's almost thirty-five now—nobody can call her an impressionable kid any more—and she's decided she wants to come back to me."

For weeks and months afterwards, Emily thought of

many passionate, well-worded rejoinders she might have made to that statement; at the time, though, all she could muster was the weak, meek little phrase she had hated herself for using since childhood: "I see."

It took only a couple of days for Howard to move his belongings out of the apartment. He was very apologetic about everything. Only once, when he flicked the heavy silken rope of his neckties out of the closet, was there any kind of a scene, and that turned into such a dreadful, squalid scene—it ended with her falling on her knees to embrace his legs and begging him, begging him to stay— that Emily did the best she could to put it out of her mind.

There were worse things in the world than being alone. She told herself that every day as she went efficiently about the business of getting ready for work, of enduring her eight hours in Baldwin Advertising and of conquering the evenings until she could sleep.

There was no longer any listing for Michael Hogan in the Manhattan Telephone Directory, or any listing for his public relations firm. He had always talked of moving to Texas, which was his home; probably he'd made the move.

Ted Banks was still listed, at his old address, but when she called him he explained with what seemed an excessive amount of embarrassment that he was married to a wonderful person.

She tried others—it had always seemed that her life was filled with men—but none came through.

There was no Flanders, John; and when she tried Flanders, J., on West End Avenue, it turned out to be a woman.

For a year she found an exquisite pain—almost pleasure

—in facing the world as if she didn't care. Look at me, she would say to herself in the middle of a trying day. Look at me: I'm surviving; I'm coping; I'm in control of all this.

But some days were worse than others; and one afternoon, a few days before her forty-eighth birthday, turned out to be especially bad. She had carried a batch of finished copy and layouts uptown for a client's approval, and on coming back she was all the way into Hannah Baldwin's office before discovering that she'd left it all on the seat of the taxicab.

"Oh, my God!" Hannah cried, reeling back on the casters of her desk chair as if she'd been shot through the heart. Then she came forward again, placed both elbows on the desk and held her head with all ten fingers, messing up her careful hair. "You've gotta be kidding," she said. "That was *finished* copy. That was *approved* copy. It had the client's *signature* on it . . ."

And Emily stood watching her, realizing at last how much she had always disliked her, knowing this was probably the last time she would ever face this humiliation.

". . . Total, utter carelessness," Hannah was saying. "Any *child* could've been trusted with a thing like this, and it's so *typical* of you, Emily. And it isn't as if you hadn't been warned; I've given you every chance. I've been carrying you—I've been carrying you for years—and I simply can't afford it any longer."

"I have several things to tell *you*, Hannah," Emily said, proud that she was shaking only a little and that her voice came out almost steady, "and the first is that I've worked here too long to be 'fired.' I want to resign as of today."

Hannah took her hands away from her disheveled hair and looked up into Emily's eyes for the first time. "Oh,

RICHARD YATES

Emily, you *are* a child. Don't you see I'm trying to do you a favor? If you resign you'll have nothing. If you let me fire you, you can draw Unemployment. Don't you even know that? Were you born yesterday?"

CHAPTER 3

ON THE DOLE—A WOMAN'S STORY

If you're fired from a job in New York, you can receive unemployment compensation checks for fifty-two weeks. After that, if you still haven't found work, your only recourse is to go on Welfare. There are more than one and a half million people on Welfare in the metropolitan area.

I am white, Anglo-Saxon, Protestant, and a college graduate. I have always earned my living in "professional" fields—as a librarian, as a journalist, and finally as an advertising copywriter. I am now in my ninth month of unemployment status, with nothing but Welfare in sight. My employment counsellors, public and private, have done their best; they tell me there simply aren't any jobs.

Perhaps no one can fully explain this predicament, but at the risk of displaying an easy and all too fashionable self-pity, I will hazard a guess: I am a woman, and I am no longer young.

That was as far as Emily's article went. It had been rolled into her typewriter for weeks; now the paper was curled and sun-bleached and gathering dust.

She was in the eleventh month of her unemployment status when she began to fear that she might be losing her mind. She had given up the old apartment and moved into a smaller, cheaper place in the West Twenties, not far from where Jack Flanders had once lived. Watching the early morning light filter down among the loft buildings across the street, she often thought of Jack Flanders fondling her elbow inside his bathrobe and saying "Sometimes, if you play your cards right, you get to meet a nice girl." But that was part of the trouble: she lived in memories all the time. No sight or sound or smell in the whole of New York was free of old associations; wherever she walked, and she sometimes walked for hours, she found only the past.

Hard liquor frightened her, but she drank enough beer to help her sleep in the afternoons—it was a good way to kill time—and it was on waking from one of these naps, sitting on the bed and staring at four empty beer cans on the floor, that she had her first intimations of madness. If anyone had asked her what day or month or year it was she would have had to say "Wait—let me think," and she didn't know whether the gray beyond her windows was dawn or dusk. Worse still, her dreams had been filled with clamorous voices from the past, and now the voices were still talking. She ran for the door to make sure it was locked— Good; nobody could get in; she was alone and safe in her own private place—and after standing there for a long time with her fist in her mouth she got the telephone book and fumbled through the "New York—City of" listings until she found "Mental Health Information Service." But when she tried to call that number it rang eleven times with no answer. Then she remembered it was Sunday; she would have to wait.

"You ought to get out and *meet* people, Emily," Grace Talbot often told her. Grace Talbot had worked at Baldwin Advertising too, until she found a better job with a bigger agency, and lately had become Emily's only friend. She was wry and hawk-faced and not very likable, but once a week, when they met for a restaurant dinner together, she seemed better than nothing.

And she was certainly better than nothing now. Emily was halfway through the dialing of her number before she realized she didn't know what to say. She couldn't say "Grace, I think I'm going crazy" without sounding like a fool.

"Hello?"

"Hi, Grace, it's Emily. I just called for—you know—no very good reason, except to talk."

"Oh. Well, that's—nice. How've you been?"

"Oh, okay, I guess, except that Sundays in New York can be pretty awful."

"Really? God, I *love* Sundays. I luxuriate in bed for hours with the *Times*, and with cinnamon toast and cups upon cups of tea, and then in the afternoon I take a walk in the park, or sometimes friends drop over, or sometimes I go to a film. It's the only day of the week when I really feel like myself."

There was a pause during which Emily regretted having called at all. Then she said "What'd you do this afternoon?"

"Oh, I had a drink with some friends, George and Myra

Fox. *I've* told you about them: he writes blurb copy for paperback books; she's a commercial artist. They're delightful people."

"Oh. Well, I just thought I'd check in with you and—you know—see what you were up to." Everything she said made her hate herself more and more. "I'm sorry if I bothered you in the middle of something, or anything like that."

And there was another pause. "Emily?" Grace Talbot said at last. "You know something? I wish you'd quit kidding me, and quite kidding yourself. *I* know how lonely you are; it's a *crime* for anyone to be that lonely. Listen: George and Myra are having a few people over next Friday evening. How about coming along with me? . . ."

A party. It would be the first party in longer than she wanted to remember, and Friday was only five days away.

All week she could think of nothing else; then Friday was upon her, and all that mattered in the world was getting her clothes and her hair right. She settled on a simple black dress (She couldn't help remembering how Howard Dunninger had said, of Linda, "She was wearing a simple, short black dress . . .") and a hair style that left one lock attractively low over the eye. She looked good. There might easily be a man there, a graying, pleasant-looking man of her own age or older, who would say "Tell me about yourself, Emily . . ."

But it wasn't really a party at all. The eight or ten people in the Foxes' living room never left their seats to get up and move around; they all seemed to know each other, and they sat in attitudes of exhaustion, with sardonic faces, sipping at tiny glasses of cheap red wine. There were no unattached men. Emily and Grace, sitting well apart from the main group, were wholly excluded from the talk until Myra Fox bustled over to their rescue, bringing the expectant listening looks of several other guests in her wake.

"Have I told you about Trudy?" she demanded of Grace. "Our neighbor on this floor? She said she might drop in later, so you may meet her, but you really ought to *know* about her first. She's really something. She's—"

And here George Fox, standing with a wine bottle poised for pouring, interrupted his wife in a voice loud enough to address the group. "Trudy runs a women's masturbation clinic," he said.

"Oh, George, it's not a 'clinic.' It's a studio."

"A studio, right," George Fox said. "She gets women of all ages—mostly sort of middle-aged, I gather—and she charges quite a hefty fee. The classes meet in her studio and go through a warm-up of modern dance routines—in the nude, of course—and then they get down to the—well, they get down to the business at hand, you might say. Because Trudy doesn't believe in masturbation as a poor substitute for the real thing, you see; she believes in masturbation as a way of life. Sort of the ultimate in radical feminism. Who needs men?"

"I don't believe it," somebody said.

"You don't believe it? Stick around. You'll meet her. Ask her yourself. And she likes nothing better than to show visitors through the studio."

Trudy did drop in later—or rather, she made an entrance. The most startling thing about her was that her head was shaved—she looked like a handsome, totally bald man of forty or so—and then you noticed her clothes: a man's purple undershirt through which the nipples of her small breasts jutted, and a pair of well-bleached blue jeans whose crotch had been appliquéd in the pattern of a big yellow butterfly. She mingled with the company for a while, drawing deeply on a cigarette in a way that emphasized her hollow cheeks and prominent cheekbones; then, when some of the guests were beginning to leave, she said "Would anyone care to see my studio?"

First came an entrance hall with many coat hooks on its walls and a sign above its archway reading PLEASE REMOVE YOUR CLOTHES. "You can ignore that," Trudy said, "but please do take off your shoes," and she led her stockinged visitors into the big, deeply carpeted main room.

On one wall was a huge, anatomically perfect drawing of a woman reclining naked with her legs apart, fondling one breast with one hand and applying an electric vibrator to her crotch with the other. On another wall, bathed in a spotlight from the ceiling, was what looked like a sculptured sunburst of many podlike aluminum shapes. Close up, the pods proved to be precise life-sized renderings of open vaginas—some considerably larger than others, all with intricately different kinds of outer and inner labia. Emily was inspecting the display when Trudy came up to stand at her shoulder.

"These are some of my students," she explained. "A sculptor friend of mine modeled them in wax, then they were cast into aluminum."

"I see," Emily said. "Well, that's very—interesting." The glass of wine was warm and sticky in her fingers, and her spine ached with tiredness. She had a presentiment that if she didn't get out of here at once, Trudy would invite her to enroll in her classes.

Trying not to hurry, she excused herself and went back to the entrance hall where her shoes lay, and then back to the Foxes' apartment where several people were agreeing with each other that Trudy's studio was the God damnedest thing they had ever seen.

"I *told* you," George Fox kept saying. "You wouldn't believe me, but I *told* you . . ."

Then the party was over and she was out on the sidewalk saying goodnight to Grace Talbot, who insisted several times that the evening had been "fun," and then she was on her way home.

There were no more parties, and she got out of the habit of taking walks. She left her apartment only to buy food ("TV dinners" and other cheap, processed food, easy to prepare and quick to eat), and there were many days when she didn't even do that. Once, having willed herself out on the street and into a corner delicatessen, she had selected her purchases from the shelves and the freezer and placed them near the cash register when she looked up and found the proprietor smiling into her eyes. He was a soft, stout man in his sixties, with coffee stains on his apron, and in none of the times she'd dealt with him before had he ever smiled like that, or even spoken to her.

"You know something?" he said, as shyly as if he were about to make a declaration of love. "If all my customers were like you, my life would be a great deal happier."

"Mm?" she said. "Why is that?"

"Because you help yourself," he said. "You pick everything out for yourself and you bring it up here. That's wonderful. Most people—especially the women—come in here and say 'Box of Wheaties.' I go all the way back to where the cereal's kept, bring it all the way back up, and they say 'Oh, I forgot—a box of Rice Krispies, too.' So for thirty-nine cents I'm getting a heart attack. Not you. Not you, ever. You're a pleasure to do business with."

"Well," she said. "Thank you." And her fingers trembled as she counted out the dollar bills. It was the first time in nearly a week that she'd heard the sound of her own voice, and it had been much, much longer than that since anyone —anyone—had said something nice to her.

Several times she started to dial the number for Mental Health Information Service, but couldn't make herself complete the call. Then once she did complete it and was referred to another number, at which a woman with a heavy Spanish accent, speaking carefully, explained the procedure: Emily could go to Bellevue Hospital any weekday morning before ten, go down to the basement level and look for a sign reading WALK-IN CLINIC. There she would be interviewed by a social worker, and an appointment with a psychiatrist would be arranged for her at a later date.

"Thank you very much," Emily said, but she never went. The prospect of going down into the bowels of Bellevue in search of the Walk-in Clinic seemed almost as bereft of hope as that of walking into Trudy's studio.

One afternoon she was returning from a long walk to the Village that she'd forced herself to take—a visit seething with memories of the dead—when she came to a stop on the sidewalk and felt her blood quicken with the beginnings of a new idea. She hurried home then, and once she was alone behind her locked door she dragged a heavy, dusty cardboard box out of its storage place and into the middle of the floor. It was a box of old letters—she had never been able to throw a letter away—and she went through many thick handfuls of shifting, sliding envelopes, all of them hopelessly out of chronological order, before she found one of the two she was looking for:

Mr. and Mrs. Martin S. Gregory
Have the honor to announce the marriage of their daughter
Carol Elizabeth
to
The Reverend Peter J. Wilson
On Friday, the eleventh of October, nineteen sixty-nine
St. John's Church
Edwardstown, New Hampshire

She remembered being slightly hurt at not having been invited to the wedding, but Howard had said "Oh, that's silly; nobody gives big, fancy weddings any more." She had sent an expensive silver gift and received a nice, touchingly young-sounding note of thanks from Peter's bride, written in a bold little private-school hand.

It took what seemed hours to find the second item, which was a good deal more recent.

The Reverend and Mrs. Peter J. Wilson
Announce the birth of a daughter
Sarah Jane
Seven pounds, six ounces
December third, nineteen seventy

"Oh, look, Howard," she had said. "They named her after Sarah. Isn't that nice?"

"Mm," he'd said. "Very nice."

But now that she had the two announcements she wasn't certain what to do with them. To hide the uncertainty from herself she spent a long time cleaning up the spilled, strewn letters on the floor and stuffing them back into the box, which she heaved and skidded back into the shadows where it belonged. Then she washed the dust off her hands and sat quiet with a cold can of beer, trying to think.

It was four or five days before she worked up the courage to place a person-to-person call to the Reverend Peter J. Wilson in Edwardstown, New Hampshire.

"Aunt Emmy!" he said. "Wow, it's good to hear from you. How've you been?"

"Oh, I've been—all right, thanks. And how are all of you? How's the little girl?"

And they went on that way, talking of nothing at all, until he said "You still at the advertising agency?"

"No, I—actually, I haven't been doing that for some time. Actually, I'm not working at all now." She was keenly aware of having said "actually" twice, and it made her bite her lip. "I'm just sort of living alone now, and I've got a lot of time on my hands, which I guess is why"—she tried a little laugh—"which I guess is why I just decided to call you up out of the blue."

"Well, great," he said, and the way he said "great" made it clear that he'd understood what "just sort of living alone now" meant. "That's great. You ever get up this way?"

"What's that?"

"Do you ever get up this way? New England? New Hampshire? Because I mean we'd love to see you. Carol's always wanted to meet you. Maybe you could come up for a weekend or something. Wait, listen: *I've* got an idea. How about *next* weekend?"

"Oh, Peter—" Her heart was beating rapidly. "—Now it sounds like I've invited myself."

"No, no," he insisted. "Don't be silly—it doesn't sound like that at all. Listen. We've got plenty of room; you'd be perfectly comfortable—and it doesn't have to be just for the weekend, either; you can stay as long as you like. . . ."

It was arranged. She would ride up to Edwardstown on the bus the following Friday—it was a six-hour trip, with an hour's layover in Boston—and Peter would meet her at the station.

For the next few days she moved with a new authority, a sense of herself as someone important, someone to be reckoned with, someone to love. Clothes were a problem: she had so few that were suitable for New England in the spring that she toyed with the idea of buying more, but that was silly; she couldn't afford it. On the night before her journey she stayed up late to wash out all her underwear and pantyhose under the weak yellow light of the bathroom (the landlord had economized by installing twenty-five-watt bulbs in all the bathrooms) and after that she couldn't sleep. She was still frazzled with lack of sleep when she carried her small suitcase into the raucous labyrinth of the Port Authority Bus Terminal, early Friday morning.

She had thought she might sleep on the bus, but for a long time all she could do was smoke many cigarettes and stare through her blue-tinted window at the passing landscape. It was a brilliant April day. Then a spasm of sleep took her by surprise in the early afternoon; she awoke with a cramp in one arm, with her dress badly wrinkled and her eyeballs feeling as if they'd been sprinkled with sand. The bus was only a few minutes from Edwardstown.

Peter's greeting was enthusiastic. He grabbed up her suitcase as if the sight of her carrying such a load offended him, and led her off toward his car. It was a pleasure to walk beside him: he moved in an easy, athletic stride and held her elbow with his free hand. He was wearing his clerical collar—she thought he must be a very high-church Episcopalian, if he wore it all the time—with a rather natty light gray suit.

"The country's beautiful up here," he said as he drove. "And you really picked a beautiful day to arrive."

"Mm. It's lovely. It certainly was—nice of you to ask me."

"It was nice of you to come."

"Is your house far from here?"

"Only a few miles." After a while he said "You know something, Aunt Emmy? I've thought of you often since this Women's Lib movement began. You've always struck me as the original liberated woman."

"Liberated from what?"

"Well, you know—from all the old, outmoded sociological concepts of what a woman's role should be."

"Jesus, Peter. I hope you do better than *that* in your sermons."

"Better than what?"

"Using phrases like 'outmoded sociological concepts.' What are you—one of these 'hip' priests?"

"Oh, I guess I'm fairly hip, yes. You have to be, if you're working with young people."

"How old are you now, Peter? Twenty-eight? Twenty-nine?"

"You *are* out of touch, Aunt Emmy. I'm thirty-one."

"And how old is your daughter?"

"Going on four."

"I was—very pleased," she said, "that you and your wife named your daughter after your mother."

"Good," he said, pulling out into the passing lane to overtake a fuel truck. When he'd drawn back into the driving lane he said "I'm glad you were pleased. And I'll tell you what: we're hoping for a boy next time, but if we have another girl we might name her after you. What would you think of that?"

"Well, I'd be very—that would be very—" But she couldn't finish because she was collapsed and crying against the passenger's door, hiding her face with both hands.

"Aunt Emmy?" he inquired shyly. "Aunt Emmy? You okay?"

This was humiliating. She hadn't been with him ten minutes, and already she had let him see her cry. "I'm fine," she said as soon as she could speak. "I'm just—tired, is all. I didn't get much sleep last night."

"Well, you'll sleep tonight. The air is very thin and very pure up here; people say it makes them sleep like the dead."

"Mm." And she busied herself with lighting a cigarette, the ritual she had relied on all her life to restore an illusion of composure.

"My mother used to have trouble sleeping," he said. "I remember when we were kids we were always saying 'Be quiet. Mom's trying to sleep.' "

"Yes," Emily said. "I know she had trouble sleeping." She was keenly tempted to say How did she die? but controlled herself. Instead she said "What's your wife like, Peter?"

"Well, you'll meet her soon enough. You'll get to know her."

"Is she pretty?"

"Oh, wow, is she ever. She's beautiful. I guess like most men I've always had fantasies of beautiful women, but this girl's a fantasy come to life. Wait'll you see her."

"All right. I'll wait. And what do you do, the two of you? Do you sit around talking about Jesus all the time?"

"Do we what?"

"Do you stay up late talking about Jesus and resurrection and stuff like that?"

He glanced briefly at her, looking puzzled. "I don't see what you're getting at."

"I'm only trying to get some picture of your—of how you—of the way you spend your time with your fantasy come to life." She could hear hysteria rising in her voice. She rolled down the partly opened window and snapped her cigarette away into the windstream, and all at once she felt strong and exhilarated, the way she'd felt in confronting Tony. "So all right, Mr. Wonderful," she said, "let's come clean. How did she die?"

"I don't even know what you're—"

"Peter, your father used to beat your mother all the time. That's a thing I happen to know, and I know you know it too. She told me all three of you boys knew it. Don't lie to me; how did she die?"

"My mother died of a liver ailment—"

"—'complicated by a fall she took in the house.' Oh, I've heard that song and dance before. You kids must've really memorized that line. Well, it's the *fall* I want to hear about. How did she fall? How was she hurt?"

"I wasn't there, Aunt Emmy."

"Christ, what a cop-out. You weren't there. And you never even asked?"

"Of course I asked. Eric was there; he told me she stumbled over a chair in the living room and struck her head."

"And do you really think that's enough to kill somebody?"

"It could be, sure, if the person falls badly."

"All right. Tell me about the police investigation. I happen to know there was a police investigation, Peter."

"There's *always* an investigation in a case like that. They didn't find anything; there was nothing to find. You sound like some kind of—why're you grilling me, Aunt Emmy?"

"Because I want to know the truth. Your father is a very brutal man."

Trees and neat white houses streamed past the car window, with a blue-green range of mountains high in the distance, and Peter took his time in answering her—so much time that she began to be afraid he was looking for a place to turn the car around, so he could drive her back to the bus station and send her home.

"He's a limited man," he said at last, speaking carefully, "and in many ways an ignorant man, but I wouldn't call him brutal."

"Brutal," she insisted, trembling badly now. "He's brutal and stupid and he killed my sister—he killed her with twenty-five years of brutality and stupidity and neglect."

"Come on, Aunt Emmy; cut it out. My father's always done the best he could. Most people do the best they can. When terrible things happen, there usually isn't anyone to blame."

"What's *that*, for God's sake? Is that something you learned in your seminary, along with 'Turn the other cheek'?"

He had slowed down and signaled to make a turn, and now she saw a short concrete driveway, a neat lawn, and a small two-story house of exactly the kind she had imagined. They were here. The inside of the garage, where he brought the car to a stop, was tidier than most people's garages. Leaning against the wall were two bicycles, one with a padded baby seat attached behind its saddle.

"So you bicycle!" she called to him across the top of the car. She had gotten out quickly, still trembling, and snatched her suitcase from the back seat, then, because a good loud sound was needed to punctuate her rage, she slammed the car door with all her strength. *"That's* what you do. Oh, and what a lovely sight it must be, the two of you out bicycling with little what's-her-name on a Sunday afternoon, all tanned and leggy in your sexy little cut-off jeans—you must be the envy of all New Hampshire...." She had started around the back of the car to join him, but he was only standing there and looking at her, blinking.

"... And then you come home and take showers—do you take showers together?—and maybe you play a little grab-ass in the kitchen while you're fixing drinks, and then you have dinner and put the baby to bed and sit around talking about Jesus and resurrection for a while, and then comes the main event of the day, right? You and your wife go into the bedroom and shut the door, and you help each other take off all your clothes, and then oh, Lord God— talk about fantasies coming to *life*—"

"Aunt Emmy," he said, "that's out of line."

Out of line. Breathing hard, with her jaws clenched tight, she carried her suitcase down the driveway toward the street. She didn't know where she was going and she knew she looked ridiculous, but it was impossible to walk in any other direction.

At the foot of the driveway she stopped, not looking back, and after a while she heard a jingle of pocketed coins or keys and a rubber-heeled tread; he was coming down to get her.

She turned around. "Oh, Peter, I'm sorry," she said, not quite looking at him. "I can't—I can't tell you how sorry I am."

He seemed very embarrassed. "You don't have to apologize," he said, taking the suitcase from her hand. "I think you're probably very tired and need some rest." He was looking at her in a detached, speculative way now, more like an alert young psychiatrist than a priest.

"Yes, I'm tired," she said. "And do you know a funny thing? I'm almost fifty years old and I've never understood anything in my whole life."

"All right," he said quietly. "All right, Aunt Emmy. Now. Would you like to come on in and meet the family?"